First Contact

"If you can go outside, please do so," said the blue woman.

I don't like to go outside if I can help it. But I went. So did Mom. So did most of the people in our development. A humming sound filled the sky. I looked up and gasped.

The sky was filled with enormous red ships. They hovered there, not moving, as if suspended by invisible cables.

"This is the Vegan Starfleet," boomed the voice, which now seemed to come directly from the sky. "It comes in peace."

If you come in peace, then why are there so many of you? I wondered.

Other Avon Camelot Books
Compiled and Edited by
Bruce Coville

BRUCE COVILLE'S SHAPESHIFTERS

Coming Soon

BRUCE COVILLE'S STRANGE WORLDS

BRUCE COVILLE'S
ALIEN VISITORS

COMPILED AND EDITED BY
BRUCE COVILLE

ASSISTED BY ELIZABETH SKURNICK

Illustrated by Alex Sunder and John Nyberg

A GLC BOOK

AN AVON CAMELOT BOOK

AVON BOOKS, INC.
1350 Avenue of the Americas
New York, New York 10019

CONTENTS

INTRODUCTION:

Just Visiting!

Did you ever look at your family, your classroom, your world and think, "Good grief! What am I doing here? I must have come from somewhere else!"

I suspect we all have that feeling at some time in our lives—the feeling that we don't fit in, don't belong, that we're so out of place it's as if we come from another planet. Which may be one reason that so many of us are fascinated by stories about people (or creatures, or bug-eyed monsters) that *do* come from other planets. We can imagine exactly how they feel!

This is especially true when we're kids, and the world hasn't yet had a chance to squeeze our own weirdness out of us. We may even like to think, "Ah! These are my people! Maybe they've come to take me home at last."

That's why I thought it would be fun to collect a book full of stories about alien visitors. Which is what you are holding now. In the pages that follow, you will find stories about aliens who have come to our planet for all sorts of purposes. Some are fierce, some friendly, some just plain weird. Some of the authors of these stories, like Ray Bradbury, turn the entire idea on its head, and show us something different altogether. Others, like Sherwood Smith, talk about how aliens might react to us. Still others, such as Lou

Grinzo, discuss how we might react to the aliens.

Fourteen stories.

Fourteen ways to think about alien visitors.

If, like me, you believe the day will come when we find ourselves face to face with visitors from another world, stories like these are not only fun to read, they also offer a way to think in advance about how we're going to feel, and act, when those aliens finally arrive.

Not a bad idea to do some advance thinking for what may be the most important day in the history of the planet.

So there you are. We've got a spaceship full of aliens waiting to meet you . . . and it's ready to land, just as soon as you turn the page.

THE LITTLE FINGER OF THE LEFT HAND

by Mel Gilden

The old guy stood in the lounge looking out through the big picture window at the kids bounding across the surface of the Moon. Even in their bulky suits the old guy could tell them apart: red suit for Arthur, blue suit for Beatrice, and yellow suit for Little Dan. Ms. Fosdick, in her conservative brown suit, was leading them.

Ms. Fosdick hurried them in through the public airlock, and as the kids removed their helmets their argumentative voices filled the lounge. Strangers looked at them, smiled, and went back to their own affairs.

"I'm not kidding! I saw an alien fossil out there," Little Dan insisted. He was a sturdy boy of seven.

At fourteen, Arthur was tall for his age. He ran a hand through his hair, but it refused to lie down. "There is no life on the Moon," Arthur said. "Never has been."

"Arthur's right," Beatrice said. "There are no aliens. Everybody knows that. What you saw was a rock formation, and *that's all*." Beatrice was only thirteen, but she was very pretty—everybody knew that, too. Her beauty gave her confidence.

"You have such imaginative grandchildren, Mr. Slatterman," Ms. Fosdick said as she smiled indulgently. She had a long thin face—like a horse, Little Dan always said when Ms. Fosdick wasn't around.

"What do *you* say, Gramps?" Little Dan asked. "Are there aliens?"

Mr. Slatterman was older than all three kids put together. "When I was not much older than you are," he said as he sat down on a long yellow couch, "I actually met some actual aliens."

Little Dan looked at him with wide-eyed wonder. Arthur and Beatrice frowned.

"I see where the children get their imagination," Ms. Fosdick said. She shook her head with disapproval.

"No, really," Mr. Slatterman said. "Aliens."

Young Howard Slatterman was lost in the big woods that surrounded his uncle Fred's cabin. He'd developed a headache from reading comic books all day, and Uncle Fred suggested that a walk in the fresh air might help. The headache was gone, but Howard would have taken it back if it came with a good map.

He walked among the big leafy trees, becoming more fearful all the time. Because he was a city boy, his sense of direction failed him in any region that wasn't paved.

"Hello!" he cried, but the wilderness seemed to swallow the sound whole.

He entertained himself by trying to decide whether he'd rather be eaten by a bear or die of starvation. Were there bears around here? Were any of these plants edible? He had no idea. Not wanting to get more lost, he sat down on a big rock. Cold came up through his jeans.

He was picking at the skin around one fingernail

when he heard the shriek of something big diving through the air, then an explosion that rattled the trees around him and the teeth in his head. Forgetting his fears for the moment, Howard leaped to his feet and glanced around. Off to his right a single spout of fire rose into the air and disappeared. Something must have crashed!

Howard ran toward it, but as he approached the crash site he became more cautious. Attempting to be both silent and invisible, he crept up on it.

He looked around the side of a big bush and saw something in a clearing—a spaceship about the size of a school bus, bent in half and smoking. It looked like a broken toy. It could have been a secret government project, Howard supposed, but he didn't think so. From the odd look of the ship, humans had not had anything to do with building it.

Howard stepped forward slowly, his fear overwhelmed by his curiosity. Were there beings on the ship? Were they alive or dead? If they were alive would they hurt him? Even if they were dead would they give him a strange alien disease?

Something clambered out of the wreckage and staggered toward him.

"Gosh!" Little Dan exclaimed.

"It was a coincidence that you were out there when that ship crashed," Arthur pointed out.

"It could have happened to anybody," Beatrice added.

"Absolutely," Mr. Slatterman agreed. "I was totally unprepared for what the guy wanted me to do."

"What was it?" Little Dan demanded.

The guy fell facedown on the ground. Howard hurried over and studied him. From this angle the guy looked human enough—two arms, two legs, a single head. He seemed to be wearing a long, brown raincoat.

Howard almost knelt to help, but he stopped, wondering how he *could* help or if he even *should* help. Howard had seen enough TV shows and movies to know that not all aliens were friendly.

Struggling, the guy turned himself over and leaned on one elbow so he could look up at Howard with large, heavy-lidded eyes. His mouth was a long slit. To Howard, the guy looked kind of like a turtle. It was not a face that was easy to read. The front of his raincoat was covered with pockets of all sizes.

"Yo," the guy said. His voice was surprisingly high and clear, like the tinkle of a little bell.

"Yo," Howard replied, hoping that was a greeting and not a war cry.

"I need your help," the guy said.

"You speak English," Howard said, astonished. After considering for a few seconds, he continued more calmly. "You've probably been monitoring our radio and TV broadcasts," he said.

"Why would we do that?" the guy tinkled. "Everybody out in the galaxy speaks English."

"They do?"

"Of course. English is a characteristic of life itself."

"You're kidding."

"No. But I don't have time to argue about it." He was wracked with a coughing fit, and when he was done he spit out a gelatinous, yellowish blob that grew frog's legs and hopped out of sight into the underbrush.

"What was that?"

"I'm badly injured," the guy said, his voice now more of a croak. He opened one of the larger pockets on the front of his raincoat and took from it a small football-shaped object. A single fin rose from one end, and lights chased each other around the long side. Every second or so it made a quiet blooping sound. To Howard's surprise, the guy handed the thing to him.

"What is this?" Howard asked.

"We haven't much time," the guy said. "I am special operative Sandar Mons of the Galactic Police. I am being followed by agents of the evil Kralndor, Zeemoo. If this McGuffin falls into Zeemoo's hands—he doesn't actually have hands, but you know what I mean—the entire galaxy will be at risk."

"And I come into this sad story where?" Howard asked, entirely mystified.

"Zeemoo's agents will be here soon. Their ship was right on my tail when I lost control in your atmosphere. Your job is to prevent them from getting the McGuffin until more Galactic Police arrive. The police will take over from there." He coughed and once again hawked up one of those tiny, gelatinous frogs.

Howard liked this situation less the more Sandar

talked. "When are the Galactic Police coming?" he asked, hoping it would be soon.

"I don't know. Soon. Maybe. You must help."

Howard was not encouraged by that. "I'm just a kid," he said. "How am I supposed to fight the agents of an alien super-bad guy?"

"With this," Sandar said. He reached out with a hand that seemed to have too many fingers and tightly gripped the front of Howard's head.

"Hey!" Howard cried and fought to get free. Suddenly, ideas began to fill his mind. They dazzled him so that he stopped fighting.

"I have given you the ability to change your form at will," Sandar said, sounding very tired, "and some simple codes that will allow you to change into several predetermined shapes—the shape of a Galactic Policeman, for instance."

"Yeah! Sure!" Howard exclaimed. "I see! This is easy!" He looked at Sandar, frowning. "But why should I trust you? For all I know, you might be the bad guy. You and the agents of Zeemoo might both be bad guys."

"Sometimes, kid, you have to go with your guts. Here." He took something else from another pocket and thrust it into Howard's hands. "It's a Lightning Five Thousand Proto Blaster. Don't kill anybody by accident." He collapsed back into the ground and shut his eyes.

"But what if—?"

Sandar waved one hand in the air briefly before it dropped to the ground.

Howard shook him frantically. "I'm just a kid!" he shouted.

Sandar began to change. The features of his face, his body shape, even his clothing began to run slowly, as if they were made of warm wax. Despite his distress, Howard could not help being fascinated.

Sandar's face morphed until it was less like a turtle's and more like an insect's. He now had a complicated mouth and big compound eyes. Altogether, he looked like a man-sized cockroach with a thick lizard tail that stuck out to one side. He wore a long jerkin that seemed to be made of woven plastic straps. Near his left shoulder was a round, midnight-blue patch with a silver needle of a spaceship that zoomed across it again and again.

"Gosh," Howard said out loud. Sandar's new shape was not one that inspired confidence. Still, he might be a Galactic Policeman after all. Maybe.

Howard was sure Sandar was dead. He stood up, the McGuffin in one hand and the proto blaster in the other, and tried to let his guts tell him what to do. His guts told him to put down the McGuffin and the weapon and walk away quickly, to forget any of this ever happened. He was sure that Sandar's intergalactic enemies were more than he could handle. Even so, he continued to stand there hefting the object in each hand.

His guts spoke again. *Wait a minute,* he advised himself. *You have a super power and a super weapon. You* can *do this.* Yes, but *should* he? Identifying the bad guys was of more than theoretical interest. If he made the wrong decision, he might endanger the entire galaxy.

He waited for his guts to give him another clue.

The sound of thunder began far away and rolled toward him like a giant bowling ball until it was so loud he had to put down the McGuffin and the blaster and insert his fingers into his ears. A moment later, a second ship dropped out of nowhere and touched down softly on the ground near the wreckage of Sandar's ship.

Howard stood up straight and thought one of the codes Sandar had taught him. A sensation came over him that he had never felt before. It was unusual, but not entirely unpleasant. He could describe it only as squirmy, but that didn't quite cover the sliding, squishing feeling of movement that went through his body as it changed shape.

His body flowed until it was somewhat taller than it had been, yet thinner and lighter. He was hard on the outside and soft on the inside. A long jerkin that seemed to be made of woven plastic straps covered his body. He flexed his new hands, an odd experience because they seemed like lobster claws, but with an extra claw on each hand.

"Cool!" he said as he caught his breath.

He hurriedly shoved the McGuffin into a pocket which seemed to be bigger on the inside than it was on the outside. The McGuffin didn't even bulge under his jerkin. He shoved the proto blaster into a holster which had bloomed at his waist.

A hole opened in the second ship and a creature stepped out onto the air in front of it. The creature looked like an intelligent bulldog. Its body was large and muscular and wore a bright yellow outfit that was tight as a superhero's uniform. Altogether, the bulldog creature looked very heroic. It looked a lot more noble than Sandar, who looked like a bug, for gosh sakes!

Did looks mean anything? Appearance was not a reliable guide when dealing with humans—when dealing with aliens it was even less certain. Howard had watched enough TV to know you could not sort the good guys from the bad guys by the bumps on their foreheads, their hairstyles, or the shapes of their ears.

When the lead bulldog neared the bottom of the invisible ramp, two more bulldogs stepped through the hole and began to descend.

Howard might look like a Galactic Policeman, but he didn't feel like one. However, as frightened as he was, he stood his ground.

"Yo," the lead bulldog said, greeting him.

"Yo," Howard replied. His voice tinkled as Sandar's had at first. He felt an odd sensation on his forehead. It took him a moment to realize that his antennae were whipping around.

"Please give us the McGuffin," the lead bulldog went on politely. When it spoke, its voice sounded like many voices which seemed to be talking through a mechanical voice box.

"I have a better idea," Howard said. "Just come along quietly and nobody'll get hurt." It was just a bluff, of course. Howard had no idea where the bulldogs should come along *to*. Or in *what*. Howard pulled his proto blaster and the bulldog froze.

"If you are truly a Galactic Policeman you will not shoot us," the bulldog said. The three bulldogs stepped forward.

"If?" Howard cried, feeling queasy all over. "Aren't you guys sure?"

The bulldogs huddled. A moment later they broke up and the lead bulldog stepped forward. "We are sure," he said. "*We* are the police. Please give us the McGuffin. It is the right thing to do." The bulldog was firm but still pleasant.

If Howard did not want the game to be over right now, before he figured out what was going on, he had no choice. He fired at the ground in front of the first bulldog. Howard and all three of the bulldogs jumped when the blaster spit a lightning bolt—not a real lightning bolt like one would see in the sky, but a brilliant, jagged projectile like the lightning bolt one might see in a comic strip. It struck the ground with a loud boom and kicked up clods of dirt as it burst into sparkles that disappeared at they settled.

Howard was inclined to fire again just for the entertainment value of it, but he controlled himself. A Galactic Policeman probably wouldn't do a thing like that, if that's what he was.

The lead bulldog held up one hand, and for the first time Howard saw that it had a thumb at either end. "We don't want to hurt you," he said, "but we must have the McGuffin."

Howard didn't want them to hurt him, either. "I'm sorry," was all he said.

"Very well," the lead bulldog said. He made his thumbs touch. Howard leaped aside as a blast of green fire shot out from where the thumbs touched and struck the ground where he had been standing. "Please give us the McGuffin."

"In the name of the Galactic Police . . . " Howard began, hoping for the best. He watched in horror as his blaster arm sagged like taffy at the elbow. He could feel himself melting. "Oops," he said to himself.

"Now we are certain that you are not a Galactic Policeman," the lead bulldog said, and fired another green blast.

As best he could, Howard ran into the woods, his limbs feeling like rubber. As his body softened, running became more difficult. Soon he was slithering over the rough ground, pseudopod over pseudopod, like a giant ameba. The bulldog things were not far behind.

Howard thought another code that Sandar had given him, and he found himself unable to move. His arms stretched upward, divided and divided again. As he had intended he was now a tree. He could still see and hear from a place somewhere among the leaves and branches.

The three bulldogs strode right by him without even slowing down, their thumbs at the ready. They returned a short time later, grumbling, and stopped under him, still glancing around. "Nobody makes a fool out of us," the lead bulldog said. "If we don't find him soon we must destroy the planet."

"If we destroy the planet the McGuffin goes with it,"

another bulldog said. "We dare not go home empty-handed."

"Nobody makes a fool of Feklar," the lead bulldog reminded his assistant. They walked back to the clearing in which their ship had landed.

Howard didn't like the sound of that. "Destroy the planet" might just be a figure of speech, but he didn't want to take any chances. Would the good guys think it was a fair trade—destroy the Earth to save the universe? Maybe. Maybe they were even right to think that way. But Howard had a lot of friends on Earth. And his comic book collection. And there were a few movies he hadn't seen yet. If the Earth was gone he personally wouldn't have much use for the rest of the universe.

He didn't know if he could stop them permanently, but he knew he could stop them temporarily if he went back to the clearing. He couldn't go as a tree, however, and he didn't think Feklar would buy his Galactic Police form now, even if he'd bought it before. Howard chuckled at what he decided to do.

He made himself a little shorter and a lot more muscular. His tail thrashed from side to side and he bellowed as he entered the clearing in the shape of a Tyrannosaurus *rex*—one sporting a very un-T-*rex* pair of antennae.

The three bulldogs seemed surprised.

"This is my real form," Howard roared. "Go back and report that you failed or die here and now!" He aimed his blaster at them, hoping he would not have to fire. He had never killed anything bigger than a fly.

"I'm afraid that's unacceptable," Feklar said. "Give us

the McGuffin." They readied their thumbs. Apparently, given a choice, Feklar would rather take home the McGuffin than destroy the Earth.

This was a frustrating situation. Howard considered giving up the McGuffin to save the Earth. After all, this wasn't *his* fight. And if these bulldogs were the good guys, they *deserved* the McGuffin. On the other hand, the bulldogs might be the bad guys, and if they destroyed the universe the Earth would probably go with it. Giving up the McGuffin wouldn't buy Howard anything. All this upping and backing was driving him crazy.

Howard could barely believe it when, at that moment, a loud thump filled the clearing as a third ship suddenly appeared on the ground. It was bright red and covered with tiny shards of white crystal. The ship looked like a gumdrop, a cherry gumdrop. Were the Galactic Police aboard? If they were, was that a good thing?

"Feklar!" The entire ship vibrated, making the word boom through the clearing. "Put down your thumbs and back away from the policeman."

"Careful, men," cried Feklar. "It's another trick!"

"No tricks," the ship vibrated. A cockroach dressed as Howard was walked out from behind the ship holding an object in one hand. It might have been a weapon, but it didn't look like the proto blaster. "I am Khar Nolo," the cockroach said. "Put down your thumbs and back away from the policeman."

The two bulldogs who had been following Feklar around trained their thumbs on the new arrival. Feklar kept his attention on Howard.

"Give me the McGuffin," Khar Nolo demanded and held one claw out to Howard.

"Give it to me," Feklar suggested.

"Sandar would have wanted you to give it to me," Khar Nolo said.

That was no doubt true, but knowing what Sandar wanted did not make Howard's choice any easier. He still didn't know which group was the bad guys. His guts were silent. "That's a good argument," was all he said.

"Give me the McGuffin or I'll be forced to destroy your world," Feklar said.

"That's a good argument, too," Howard agreed. It was difficult to nod because his head was connected directly to his body. An idea came to him, and his antennae whipped around.

"I'll tell you what," Howard said as he took a few steps forward. "I can't decide who to give the McGuffin to, so I'll just have to destroy it." He set the McGuffin on the ground and stepped back.

Feklar stepped toward it, but Howard waved his blaster at him. "Uh uh uh," he said, cautioning Feklar. When Feklar retreated Howard aimed at the McGuffin.

"No!" Feklar cried. Khar Nolo said nothing.

"Yes," Howard said and fired at the McGuffin. At the same moment, a lightning bolt kicked up dirt just to one side of it, and all three bulldogs screamed.

"That answers my question," Howard said as he picked up the McGuffin and tossed it to Khar Nolo. Khar Nolo caught it in one claw with leisurely skill. "I knew,"

Howard explained, "that the good guys wouldn't mind losing the McGuffin as long as the bad guys didn't get it."

Feklar and his friends were backing toward their ship.

"Absolutely," Khar Nolo said. He quickly adjusted the McGuffin, aimed it at the bulldogs, and fired. They were surrounded by a rainbow bubble which immediately shrank to a transparent sphere no larger than a baseball. Khar Nolo picked up the sphere and showed it to Howard. Inside, the three bulldogs were pounding on the wall.

"Cool," Howard said.

"Very cool," Khar Nolo agreed. "Now I have one more thing to do."

"What's that?"

Khar Nolo surprised Howard by gripping his antennae with one three-clawed hand. "Huh?" Howard cried, fearing that he'd chosen the wrong group after all.

Suddenly Howard forgot how to shapeshift. Knowing how to do it was like having a word at the tip of his tongue, like almost knowing a date he needed for a history test, like not quite remembering a dream, even as it faded. All by itself his body flowed into its normal shape. He looked down at his familiar arms and body. His head felt right, too.

"Thank you for your help," Khar Nolo said. "The galaxy will sleep a little bit safer tonight."

"That's okay. But I wish you'd left me the shapeshifting ability. Some kind of souvenir would have been nice."

"Fear not," Khar Nolo said. He lifted the body of

Sandar Mons of the Galactic Police and carried it into his cherry gumdrop ship. The ship rose into the air, making no more noise than the soft summer wind in the trees, and the other two ships rose behind it. When they reached the level of the treetops, all three ships suddenly disappeared.

Howard realized that he should have asked Khar Nolo to take him home. Not only would that have gotten him home, but he would have had a ride in a real spaceship.

But no. What a doofus.

Now all he could do was go with his guts.

"Did you find your way home, Mr. Slatterman?" Ms. Fosdick asked with some concern.

"Nope," the old guy said. "Uncle Fred had to find me with dogs." He chuckled.

The three children laughed, delighted that the story had no moral, but Ms. Fosdick seemed unsure what she ought to think.

"What souvenir did Khar Nolo leave you?" Little Dan asked.

"He didn't leave any souvenir, silly," Beatrice said. "It's just a story."

"Is it just a story?" Little Dan asked.

"Of course it is," Arthur said.

"Of course it isn't," Mr. Slatterman said. "As it turned out, Khar Nolo didn't entirely take away my ability to shapeshift." He held up the little finger of his left hand.

17

Ms. Fosdick and the three children looked at the finger doubtfully.

It began to change as if things under the skin were moving.

"Eew!" all three children cried.

Soon the little finger of Mr. Slatterman's left hand formed into a cockroach wearing a jerkin made of straps. It waved its antennae at them. Ms. Fosdick and the children got very quiet.

Mr. Slatterman put both hands into his pockets. "I think we should go home now. Your parents are probably back from shopping."

"Maybe we should take another look at that rock where Dan says he saw the fossil," Beatrice said.

"Tomorrow," Ms. Fosdick said firmly.

ALIEN GROUND

by Lois Tilton

How it started:

Derrick's room filled with an eerie, pale green light. A voice spoke from some place just inside his head, behind his ear: *Do you want to come with us? We need people like you.*

Derrick sat up in his bed but there was no one to be seen, only the light, which pulsed faintly with a sound like wind disappearing down a very deep, very distant tunnel. But he figured he knew who they were. What they were.

He thought briefly of school, of his parents, who wouldn't ever know where he'd gone. "But it serves them right." Because Derrick wasn't in his room of his own free choice. He was grounded for the whole weekend on charges that were untrue, or at least unfair. Who would want to hang around in a place where there was no TV, no games to play?

"Sure," he told the voice. "I'll go along."

What Derrick expected, more or less:

That the aliens would use some kind of beam to bring him up to the spaceship, that there'd be a command bridge full of flashing lights and strange beings and more wonders than he could even imagine.

Why Derrick supposed the aliens needed him:

Because no one else could help them defeat their enemies. Because no one, absolutely no one was better at computer combat games than Derrick Rothermel. Space combat games, street fighter games, naval warfare games—he was the best. Now the aliens were going to hook him up to their combat laser computers and have him blast away at their evil opponents.

In short:

Derrick had spent way too much time watching TV.

What really happened next:

#2

The green light started to grow brighter, so bright that Derrick had to close his eyes, and still it was blinding him. And at the same time, the wind started to pull him into the tunnel in space, whistling all the time in his ears, stretching him—stretching him out so far that he felt like he had no weight at all, and his head was all the way across the universe while his feet were still back on Earth.

Then there was a kind of *snap*, and he opened his eyes and found himself sitting on his own bed, in his own room.

"Hey!" he said, looking around, blinking in confusion. What was going on? Had it just been a dream? Well, it must have been a dream. Here he still was, in his stupid room. Grounded for the whole weekend with nothing to do! For a moment he wished the aliens really would come and take him away. Out of this place. Anywhere.

Until the voice in his head spoke again: *Welcome. Please go on about your daily routine as usual.*

Then Derrick started to be scared. Either he was crazy, or someone was playing a mean trick, or . . .

Really scared.

"Hey! What's going on?" he demanded, but his voice squeaked like a frightened little kid's.

The voice in his head had only repeated: *Welcome. Please go on about your daily routine as usual.*

Derrick jumped off his bed, looked around the room frantically. This *was* his room. His bed, with the stain on the quilt, the desk in the corner with his homework and his magazines, the laundry basket full of clothes that he hadn't put away. His movie posters on the ceiling. All his stuff, just the same.

Except—the window. He remembered (he was almost sure he remembered) the blinds had been closed, before. Now, they were open.

Suddenly, Derrick didn't want to see what was behind that window. He spun around, ran for the door.

It was locked.

Derrick lost it. He jerked and pulled on the doorknob; he kicked the door, screaming, "Hey! Let me out of here! Mom! Mom! Come open the door!"

But no one answered. No one but the voice in his head, repeating: *Please go on about your daily routine as usual.*

What Derrick really wanted to do next:

Cry.

And scream for his parents to come and get him out of this place.

Why he didn't do it:

Because he didn't want to act like a little kid while they were watching him.

And he knew, down to the cold lump in his gut, that they were watching him.

Instead, he told himself: "Get a grip. You can figure out what's going on here. You can handle this." The door, he could see now, wasn't really a door after all. It was never meant to be opened. This really wasn't his room. He was in some other place, meant to look just like his room.

And the window . . .

Derrick really, really didn't want to turn around and look at that window. But he did it. He turned around. He made himself open his eyes. And what should have been the view down into the Nicholsons' back yard, with the deck where Amy Nicholson would sometimes come out in her bikini to get a suntan . . .

. . . was blank.

"Oh, man!" Derrick whispered, except his mouth was so dry that it came out as kind of a strangled croak. He swallowed. He took a step closer to the window. Another step. "Oh, man!"

Because it wasn't really a window there at all. Instead, it seemed to be kind of like a video screen, except that it was a darker, silvery gray color. A slowly swirling gray color, almost a little bit like clouds passing across the screen. And if you looked at it closely, very closely for a while, you could start to see *them* looking back at you.

Watching.

"No!" Derrick screamed, and he hit out at the screen, hit it with his fists, as hard as he could, not even thinking that the glass might break and cut his hands. But the glass didn't break. Of course it didn't, it wasn't glass, it was some alien material so hard and indestructible that it didn't even break when he picked up his desk chair and tried to smash through it.

"Stop it!" he cried. "Stop watching me!"

But there was nothing he could do to stop them. He was an exhibit now in some kind of alien zoo. Sealed up in this room that looked like his own room, except that the window had no blinds—

He turned around, stared back at the screen. No, the window had no blinds, it had no curtains he could close to shut off their view. But he could still do it!

Derrick went to the bottom drawer of his desk, hoping it was real, hoping the aliens had duplicated all the contents. Yes! There it was, his dad's staple gun that he wasn't supposed to use, that he especially wasn't supposed to have in his room. But right now he didn't care. He grabbed the quilt off his bed, climbed up on the chair, and stapled the quilt to the wall, covering the screen. *Now* they couldn't keep watching him!

Then he retreated back to his bed, underneath the sheet, and hid his head under the pillow. What was he going to do now? What was going to happen to him? Even if the aliens couldn't watch him anymore, he was still locked up in here, wherever this place was.

"I want to go home!" he sobbed.

The voice in his head answered him: *Please go on about your daily routine as usual.* Derrick ignored it.

Again: *Please go on about your daily routine as usual.* This time he thought it seemed kind of annoyed, and he kind of grinned a little, even as miserable as he was, because it meant the quilt had worked, they really couldn't see him now. Not that the rest of his problems were solved. His knuckles were bloody and swollen where he'd pounded on the screen to try to break it, and he was hungry, and he thought he had to go to the bathroom—but there was no bathroom here!

Please go on about your daily routine as usual.

Derrick took the pillow off his head and sat up. "I want to go home!" he demanded out loud. "I don't want to stay here in this place!"

For a moment there was no response. Then, a pale green light began to fill the room.

What Derrick hoped would happen then:

The aliens would take him back home to his real room, back home to Earth, and he would never hear from them again.

What happened instead:

The light grew brighter, and Derrick's body seemed to grow heavier and lighter all at once, stretching out to an infinite extent.

Then there was a *snap*, just like before, and he opened his eyes and found himself sitting on his own bed, in his own room. Or was he still back in the alien copy of his room? There was one way to tell, but he was afraid he was going to see the swirling gray screen instead of the familiar view from his own window.

But the voice in his head answered the question: *Welcome. Please go on about your daily routine as usual.*

"No!" Derrick cried. But it was true. It was the gray screen instead of the window, it was the false door, it was exactly the same. Except for one thing. Derrick ran to his desk to make sure, but the staple gun was gone.

Now he was mad. "I'll show you," he said under his breath, because he wasn't sure whether the aliens could really hear him or not. The voice in his head, he realized now, was only some kind of stupid recording. He shoved his bed over toward the window, until it was right next to the wall, and then, with an effort, he raised up the other end until it crashed upright, resting on the headboard, with the mattress up against the wall, blocking the window completely.

"There!" he said with some satisfaction, sitting down on the floor. That would fix them. And sure enough, the stupid recording started in his head again: *Please go on about your daily routine as usual.* "No!" he yelled out loud. "I won't! I don't want to stay here! I want to go home!"

And when it repeated the message, he even said, "You go to hell!"

But he noticed something while he was sitting there waiting to see what they were going to do next. The knuckles on both his hands had been all swollen and bloody from hitting the screen, the last time. Now, they looked perfectly normal. He flexed them, and they didn't even hurt. And that worried him.

Please go on about your daily routine as usual.

"No!"

But of course it didn't last. Eventually the green light started to fill the room again, and Derrick was being pulled into the tunnel again, stretched into infinity. Then *snap*, and there he was. Again.

And this time, he knew without checking that he was still in the same place. Only this time, the bed was fastened to the floor so that he couldn't even move it an inch.

What Derrick tried to do next:

Crawl under the bed to hide from them.

It wasn't very comfortable under there. The bed was kind of low, and there was as much dust and grunge underneath, just as there'd been back in his real room at home. But Derrick was stubborn, and he refused to come out, no matter how often the voice in his head told him to go about his daily routine. Not until the light started to turn green again.

Snap.

And there he was again. Back in the same room, sitting on the same bed, only now with some kind of force field that kept him from crawling underneath it.

Welcome. Please go on about your daily routine as usual.

"I can't!" he told it. "Don't you idiots understand? This is my bedroom! I sleep here. I do my homework here sometimes. But there's nothing else to do! I've got no TV! I've got no video games! I can't do any daily routine in here!"

Please go on about your daily routine as usual.

"Argggh!" he screamed. But of course they were idiots. Or they weren't listening. Or they didn't care.

Derrick threw his pillow across the room, straight at the window/screen. He picked up the laundry basket and threw that, too. He kicked the footboard of the bed.

Nothing happened.

He went to his desk, pulled out all the drawers, flung the contents across the room, threw the drawers, threw all the books, threw his chair. He threw the reading light and heard the lightbulb shatter. He trashed the place, wrecked everything he could get his hands on.

Nothing happened.

Sobbing with frustration and fury, he flung himself back down on the bed. The gray screen was still there, they were probably watching him, but now he didn't really care any more. He wasn't ever going to win, he wasn't ever going to get out of this place!

He hit the mattress. Then he flexed his hand, held it up for a closer look. How had it healed so fast, anyway?

What was really going on in all this? What happened to him when the green light came and he felt like he was being stretched so thin he had to disappear?

Was it a kind of time warp? Were the aliens bringing him back to the same point in the past, over and over again? Or maybe they really did take him apart and put him back together. Or maybe he wasn't real; maybe he was just a copy of himself. Maybe the real Derrick Rothermel was still back in his room on Earth. Or maybe, he thought—and now he was starting to scare himself—maybe he was just like a character in a computer game, and every time the aliens pushed the reset button, the game started all over again.

But what was the game? *Watch Derrick in His Room?* What kind of a stupid, boring game was that?

Derrick got out of bed and searched around the mess on the floor until he found a thumbtack. He used it to scratch an X on the back of his left hand. Then he sat down on his bed, with his back to the window that wasn't a window.

After a while, the light began to turn the same familiar green color, and he was being pulled apart and snapped back together again.

He opened his eyes. There he was in his room, just the way it had always been. All the mess was gone.

And his hand. He slowly lifted it so he could see.

The X had disappeared.

So it was true. He was only a copy of himself. And the aliens could copy him over and over again, as long as they felt like playing the game.

What Derrick finally realized:

The very worst possible thing had happened. Here he was, a kid from Earth, transported away into some alien dimension—just the kind of adventure he'd always hoped would happen to him.

But instead, he was in his own room. With no TV, no games, nothing to do. Grounded—forever.

Derrick wanted to
be taken away by
aliens at the
beginning of the story,
By the end, he was
very sad about
it happening.

Zoo

by Edward D. Hoch

The children were always good during the month of August, especially when it began to get near the twenty-third. It was on this day that Professor Hugo's Interplanetary Zoo settled down for its annual six-hour visit to the Chicago area.

Before daybreak the crowds would form, long lines of children and adults both, each one clutching his or her dollar, and waiting with wonderment to see what race of strange creatures the Professor had brought this year.

In the past they had sometimes been treated to three-legged creatures from Venus, or tall, thin men from Mars, or even snakelike horrors from somewhere more distant. This year, as the great round ship settled slowly to earth in the huge tri-city parking area just outside of Chicago, they watched with awe as the sides slowly slid up to reveal the familiar barred cages. In them were some wild breed of nightmare—small, horselike animals that moved with quick, jerking motions and constantly chattered in a high-pitched tongue. The citizens of Earth clustered around as Professor Hugo's crew quickly collected the waiting dollars, and soon the good Professor himself made an appearance, wearing his many-colored rainbow cape and top hat. "Peoples of Earth," he called into his microphone.

The crowd's noise died down as he continued. "Peoples of Earth, this year you see a real treat for your single dollar—the little-known horse-spider people of Kaan—brought to you across a million miles of space at great expense. Gather around, study them, listen to them, tell your friends about them. But hurry! My ship can remain here only six hours!"

And the crowds slowly filed by, at once horrified and fascinated by these strange creatures that looked like horses but ran up the walls of their cages like spiders. "This is certainly worth a dollar," one man remarked, hurrying away. "I'm going home to get the wife."

All day long it went like that, until ten thousand people had filed by the barred cages set into the side of the spaceship. Then, as the six-hour limit ran out, Professor Hugo once more took microphone in hand. "We must go now, but we will return next year on this date. And if you enjoyed our zoo this year, phone your friends in other cities about it. We will land in New York tomorrow, and next week on to London, Paris, Rome, Hong Kong, and Tokyo. Then on to other worlds!"

He waved farewell to them, and as the ship rose from the ground the Earth peoples agreed that this had been the very best Zoo yet. . . .

Some two months and three planets later, the silver ship of Professor Hugo settled at last onto the familiar jagged rocks of Kaan, and the queer horse-spider creatures filed quickly out of their cages. Professor Hugo was there to say a few parting words, and then they scurried away in a hundred different directions, seeking their homes among the rocks.

In one, the she-creature was happy to see the return of her mate and offspring. She babbled a greeting in the strange tongue and hurried to embrace them. "It was a long time you were gone! Was it good?"

And the he-creature nodded. "The little one enjoyed it especially. We visited eight worlds and saw many things."

The little one ran up the wall of the cave. "On the place called Earth it was the best. The creatures there wear garments over their skins, and they walk on two legs."

"But isn't it dangerous?" asked the she-creature.

"No," her mate answered. "There are bars to protect us from them. We remain right in the ship. Next time you must come with us. It is well worth the nineteen commocs it costs."

And the little one nodded. "It was the very best Zoo ever. . . ."

FASHION VICTIM

by Esther M. Freisner

It was my big break—an exclusive interview with the top force in U.S. fashion design, the One, the only, the Original: *Totzi!* Imitated But Never Equaled. At least that's what it said on all his business cards. As my editor kept telling me while I wrapped up my research before heading out the door, I was lucky to get it.

"Totzi doesn't talk to just anyone, Richards. As a matter of fact, he seems to have a tendency to restrict his interviews to reporters who are still wet behind the ears. And let's face it, yours are positively soaking."

I absentmindedly rubbed the back of one ear and asked, "Any idea why he does that?"

My editor shrugged. "None. Maybe he likes to give new kids a break. Hey, who cares why? Count your blessings, do the job, and be grateful—this interview will make your career."

I gave one final glance at the data on my screen. I was a good girl; I'd done my homework. Every previous interview ever written about Totzi was now neatly stored away in my laptop. I even had a special file containing any really interesting details I'd noticed while reading those articles.

Funny thing, the details: there weren't all that many, and they weren't all that interesting. Every interview the great designer ever gave tended to dwell on his work, not his life. Okay, I could understand that: some people like their privacy more than others. I understood, and yet . . . it still bothered me, somehow.

Oh well, worrying about such stuff wasn't going to help my career. In fact, if I wasted any more time on foolish thoughts and didn't get over to Totzi's showrooms to do the interview, I probably wouldn't *have* a career. I entered one last question on my laptop and left the office running.

The receptionist at House of Totzi reminded me of the lunch lady at my old elementary school, the one who always used to give me dirty looks if I made any jokes about the Mystery Meat or how many rats were in the ratatouille (which I always pronounced "rat-a-*ptooey!*"). I told her I was Tina Richards from *Le Slic* magazine, I even showed her my I.D., and she *still* glared at me as if I'd announced, "Hi, I'm your friendly neighborhood homicidal maniac. Got a minute? I brought my own chainsaw."

"Totzi is *very* busy today," she told me, biting off every word as if it tasted bitter. "He has a full schedule."

Translation: you are a cockroach. Go away.

I smiled. "I know," I said. "I'm part of it. Eleventhirty, see?"

I leaned over the desk and stabbed my finger down on the open pages of the appointment book. Actually I couldn't see where the eleven-thirty appointment slot was, so I pointed at random, but it did make the receptionist look down and find my name. She wasn't happy about that.

"Have a seat," she muttered.

I did, and it took about as much luck to find an empty chair as it did to get the interview in the first place. The reception area at House of Totzi was crowded. The receptionist was telling the truth about Totzi being very busy. This was no surprise—it was the height of the fashion show season. I was sharing the great designer's schedule with models and agents and buyers and even a number of aspiring young designers, nervously balancing their big, black portfolios full of sketches on their laps.

I glanced up at the clock on the wall. It was only a little after eleven. I'd arrived early, just in case Totzi's appointments were running fast. If so, maybe he'd agree to see me ahead of schedule, so I could squeeze in a few additional minutes with the great designer.

When his personal secretary had called to tell me I'd gotten this appointment, I was also told that it absolutely could not last longer than half an hour. At noon, Totzi had to leave the office for the convention center where the biggest fashion show of the season was going to take place. Twelve o'clock sharp—no excuses, no exceptions. I didn't argue. Why bother? His secretary made sure to remind me that with so many people for him to see and so much work for him to supervise, Totzi really had done me a humongous favor by agreeing to an interview at all.

I watched the hands of the clock inch forward. People in the reception area came and went. Most of them got three minutes in Totzi's office, although some of the luckier ones got five. I felt very special to have an entire half-hour set aside for me.

I *thought* I had an entire half-hour. The minutes ticked by, the faces in the reception area changed, eleven-thirty came and went, but my name wasn't called. I started to get antsy. I had plenty of questions prepared, but the longer I sat there, the more I realized that I'd have to cut a lot of them. I'd just set up my laptop and was jiggling it impatiently on my knees, eliminating most of my planned interview, when the receptionist growled my name.

By this time it was a quarter to twelve. I told myself that wasn't so bad, I could still fit a lot of questions into fifteen minutes. But then, just as I walked into Totzi's office and got my first up-close look at the great designer, he stood up from his desk and swept past me, out the door I'd just come in.

"I will be right back, darling," he called as he rushed off. His voice had a strange, foreign accent that I couldn't place. "Forgive me, it is an emergency." As he dashed by me in a blur, I saw that even though he had a reputation for bizarre clothing designs (some of which were a little *too* bizarre for my taste), he himself wore a simple black suit, a matching shirt, and no necktie. With a smile and a farewell wave of his hand, he was gone.

I was alone in his office. It was an impressive place, as I'd expected it to be. The walls were covered with expensive art except for the one right behind his desk that was one gigantic floor-to-ceiling window with a great view of the park. I set up my laptop and started making some notes about the office itself. Since I wouldn't have time to ask all my carefully prepared questions, a description of the great designer's office would be a good way to fill up the interview.

Suddenly, I stopped short. A disturbing thought hit me. I recalled all the interviews I'd read while preparing for this assignment. Could it be . . . ? I scrolled through my files rapidly, skimming one article after another. My suspicions were confirmed: *In every previous interview, the reporter spent more than half the article talking about Totzi's office!*

Why was that? I wondered. Could it be that I wasn't the first reporter to be given a short time slot, then to have that slot made ever shorter? Was that why there was almost nothing in the earlier articles about Totzi himself, because there'd been *no time* to ask the great designer any personal questions?

Somehow, I had the feeling that Totzi's "emergency" was only another trick to keep me shut out. I'd have to put together an article like all those that had gone before: sixty percent description of his office, thirty-five percent repetition of the "official" life story his secretary had FAXed me (a life story that didn't even say where or when he'd been born!), and maybe five percent answers to my questions, if he wound up giving me any time to ask them at all.

And I couldn't even object. I was a new reporter, still "wet behind the ears," as my editor enjoyed reminding me. Everyone kept saying how lucky I was to get this assignment. If I made any kind of a stink, it wouldn't take much for Totzi to change my luck for good. He'd spread the word to other designers that I was ungrateful, "difficult" to work with, and, in short, a pest. I'd never get another major interview, which meant there was a very good chance I'd lose my job.

So that's *why he only gives interviews to new reporters!* I realized. *We're so happy to get the work that we never notice we're actually getting nothing. And he gets to hide everything about himself while he makes it look like he's got nothing to hide. Well, guess what, Totzi? They may be your rules for interview hide-and-seek, but I don't feel like playing.*

With that, I set aside my laptop and headed straight for his desk and started snooping around. I'm a reporter—snooping's what I do. If he came in and caught me, I knew I'd be thrown out on my ear. I might even lose my job, but it didn't matter. Either I was a reporter or I was nothing, and a reporter's *real* job is to discover secrets.

Did I ever!

It was a plain manila folder like so many others. It was buried in the middle of a stack of fashion magazines shoved under his desk. I might never have found it at all if I hadn't accidentally kicked the pile while struggling to get one of Totzi's locked desk drawers open. The folder went skidding out from between two magazines, the papers in it scattering across the rug. I sprang up and pounced on them, gathering them up and taking them back to my chair for closer inspection.

There were about ten pages in the folder, all with some sort of writing on them. As soon as I saw that weird scribbling, I realized that there was something definitely strange about it.

Strange? Try *alien.*

At first I thought that the writing was Japanese or Chinese. It certainly wasn't English, and after a closer look, I got the gut feeling that it was nothing earthly. The longer I stared at it, the colder I felt. It wasn't the office temperature, it was a chill of dread. I also heard a strange, high-pitched sound. I believed it was just my imagination, but then I realized that the sound was coming from the writing itself. I put the page up to my ear, to double-check, and yes, it was the writing. It was humming—humming something that sounded like a cross between the "Macarena" and the theme from *Beverly Hills 90210,* as a matter of fact. *Talk* about alien!

If the alien script tied my belly in an icy knot, that was nothing compared to the fear I felt when I looked at . . . the drawings!

There was one on every page in that folder, all of them sketches of men's and women's fashions. I know it sounds odd, but those fashion sketches were so weird, so ultrabizarre, so downright *freaky* that they made the alien writing look almost normal by comparison. Would any sane human being wear something that grotesque? And yet I knew that once these styles were turned from sketches to actual pieces of clothing, there'd be millions of people not only ready to wear those fashions but willing to pay top dollar for the chance! I stared in horror, unable to tear my eyes away.

"Well, Ms. Richards, enjoying yourself?"

A sarcastic voice broke the spell of those fearsome drawings. I looked up sharply to see Totzi standing in front of me, an alien weapon in his hand. Too small to be a gun, it still looked capable of doing serious damage.

"You're quite right, Ms. Richards, it *is* dangerous," the great designer said, as if reading my mind. "It's a visibility reductor. If I were to shoot you with it, you would not die, but you *would* become one-dimensional."

"One-di—?"

Again, he seemed to know my question before I asked it. "You would become no wider than the thinnest line you can imagine. So very thin that no one could see it . . . or you."

"Well, everyone knows you can never be *too* thin," I replied with a sickly grin, trying to break the tension with a bad joke.

He turned for a moment and aimed the device at the pile of magazines I'd knocked over when I discovered the fatal file. There was a brief whining sound and they vanished.

"Thin enough for you?" Totzi smiled an evil smile. "You see, Ms. Richards, I am not cruel. If you decide to try being a heroine, at least you will have something to read waiting for you when I zap you through to the other side. So, unless that is your idea of happiness, I suggest you put down the Master Plan—carefully!— and come with me."

I obeyed. What choice did I have? He took a moment to dispose of the sketches the same way he'd zapped the magazines, then escorted me briskly out of his office. He linked his arm in mine so that no one could see he was holding the visibility reductor against my ribs. We strolled to the elevator as if we were the best friends in the world.

"Where are you taking me?" I whispered as we rode down to the lobby. He'd used his master key to override any requests for stops on other floors. No one could disturb us; I had no chance to escape.

"To the fashion show, darling," he replied. "It will be so much easier to deal with you there, where I will have friends to help me."

"Friends?"

"The other designers. You saw the sketches. Surely you don't believe that such outlandish clothing was ever the work of you puny earthlings?"

I couldn't help gasping in astonishment. "You mean—you mean that Earth fashions are the work of . . . aliens?"

Totzi threw back his head and laughed. "Not all Earth fashions, dear girl! We haven't been here for *that* long—only about eight hundred years, perhaps nine. I'm terrible with dates; that's why I have a secretary. Have you ever studied the history of fashion? Ah, that's a foolish question—you work for *Le Slic*. Well then, didn't you ever wonder why clothing suddenly went from being a practical way to keep the human body warm and dry to . . . something more? Something . . . silly?"

I thought about that as we left the elevator, exited the House of Totzi, and got into his waiting limo. Totzi was right. I remembered seeing old paintings of people in the Middle Ages. The women wore tall hats that made them look as if they'd grown horns. The men wore

shoes so terribly long and pointy that they had to tie
thin chains under their knees to hitch up the toes so that
they could walk without tripping.

And that was only the beginning. I also remembered
pictures of men and women wearing powdered wigs so
high that barbers had to stand on ladders to style the
tops. Some of the wigs were decorated with model ships
or miniature castles, others held cages full of live song-
birds. As the years went on, there were more ridiculous
fashions: bustles and spats and corsets and hoop skirts
and paper dresses and bell bottoms and—and—

—and what is a necktie good for, anyway?

"Why?" I asked. "Why have you done this to us?"

Totzi checked to make sure that the soundproof glass
partition between us and his driver was in place before he
replied. "Why?" he echoed as we sped through the city
streets. "To see how far you'll go. Or should I say, to see
how far you'll let yourselves be led? It's an experiment.
You see, one day we mean to invade this world, when we
get around to it. We don't need it right now, and you *have*
messed it up pretty badly, but you never know when a
fixer-upper planet will come in handy. It always pays to
plan ahead."

"I don't understand," I told him. "What does fashion
have to do with conquering Earth?"

"Well, as I said, it's an experiment: we want to find
out just how dumb you earthlings are, how ready to go
along with the crowd. My fellow designers and I are
scientists, sent here to determine whether you have any
limits when it comes to following the herd."

"Do we?" I asked. I was afraid I already knew the answer.

He laughed again, louder. "I've seen lemmings with more independence and sheep with more backbone. It's gotten to be a contest among us, trying to come up with a fashion *so* ridiculous, *so* laughable, *so* senseless that no one on Earth will buy it." He shook his head, grinning, and added, "So far, no one's won. For a while there we thought we had a winner with pre-torn jeans, but . . ." He shrugged. "When we finally decide to take over, you're going to be pushovers."

The limo came to a halt at the convention center's stage door. Totzi poked me in the side with the visibility reductor, just as a friendly reminder, and steered me backstage. The place was a traffic jam of garment racks, a jungle of clothes in every color and fabric imaginable. Incredibly tall models stalked through the confusion like tigers, followed by chattering monkey swarms of makeup artists and hairstylists.

Somehow Totzi managed to find us a tiny room, away from the chaos. "I didn't see any of my friends around when we came in, but they're probably busy putting the finishing touches on their own new styles. You're not in any hurry, are you?" He gave me a terrifying smile.

My mouth was dry with fear. "What are you going to do with me?"

"I'm not sure." Totzi looked thoughtful. "I could always simply use the visibility reductor on you, but that would be wasteful. You're a reporter. We could use your powers of media influence to further our cause . . . if we felt we could trust you."

"Oh, you can trust me, all right!" I said eagerly. (*Anything* rather than having to spend the rest of my life in the one-dimensional world with nothing but a pile of old fashion magazines to keep me company!) "I've been thinking about it and, well, what's wrong with being a fashion slave? Everyone does it. Hey, I remember back in high school when the P.T.A. suggested making us wear uniforms. The kids who protested the loudest were the same ones who wouldn't be caught dead in any clothing that wasn't absolutely solid Goth black."

"Nice try," Totzi said drily. "Of course, you'd say *anything* to keep from being sent into the one-dimensional world with nothing but a stack of old fashion magazines for company."

So he *was* telepathic! Dang!

"No, I'm not," said Totzi.

"But *we* are!" came a loud, commanding, female voice. The door to the little room flew open and Totzi and I looked up simultaneously to confront a group of five supermodels, all of them aiming pink plastic hairbrushes right at the great designer.

"Fashion police!" their leader announced as one of her minions discreetly shut the room's door behind them. "Freeze!"

Somehow I didn't think she meant me, so I took the chance and jumped away from Totzi. Unfortunately for him, Totzi reacted automatically to my escape attempt. "Stop!" he cried, raising his visibility reductor.

Five hairbrushes went off at once. Four beams of bright purple light struck the great designer, freezing him where he stood. The fifth brush only sputtered out a few pathetic blue and red sparks. The supermodel holding it looked annoyed as she examined her faulty weapon.

"Wouldn't you know it?" she remarked crossly. "Dandruff."

The leader of the commando supermodels smiled and patted me on the shoulder. "You're safe now, Tina," she said. I remembered her face from hundreds of glossy full-page fashion and cosmetics ads: her name was Vikki, and her teammates were the equally famous faces Myndi, Romi, Lynda, and Steffi (the one with the dandruff problem). I looked at Totzi, stiff and still as a statue.

"He's not . . . dead, is he?" I asked. I got brave enough to reach out with one hand and touch his arm. It felt hard as wood through the sleeve of his jacket.

Vikki shook her head. "He's only in indefinite suspended animation. Don't worry, Tina, he'll still have a career in Earth fashions—as a mannequin." The five supermodels laughed.

"You're—you're not from this planet, are you?" I asked. I already knew the answer.

"You already know the answer to that, Tina," Vikki said. "But don't worry—we mean you no harm. We come from a different world than his." She nodded at Totzi's frozen body. "We do not believe in conquering worlds that are more primitive than our own," she went on.

"We hate the idea of controlling the behavior of others," said Romi.

"We think that all alien species have the right to independence," Myndi chimed in.

"We must save you from any influence that makes you do something without thinking just because everyone else is doing it," Lynda added.

"It's like my mother always told me," Steffi said. "'If all of your friends jumped into a black hole, would you do it, too?'"

I shook hands with all of the supermodels who'd rescued me. "I can't thank you enough," I said.

"No thanks are necessary," Vikki assured me. "But if you insist, then what you can do—what you must do—is warn your fellow earthlings. Totzi's under control, but his evil allies are still out there. We can't deal with them all the way we dealt with him."

"There are too many of them," Steffi said.

"It would provoke an interplanetary war," Romi added.

"So you see, it's up to you," Myndi concluded as together they all escorted me out of the little room.

Their words were inspiring, but I'd never thought of myself as a crusading journalist before. Would I be up to the task? I glanced around backstage. A woman glided by wearing an evening gown made entirely out of aluminum foil and red feathers. A man walked past in the opposite direction dressed in a purple suit with green neon trim and shoulders so wide you could skateboard off them. The aliens were right: this *was* evil, and it had to be stopped!

"I'll *do* it!" I declared. "I'm going to use my power as a reporter to get out the message that thinking for yourself, respecting yourself, *being* yourself is way more important than blindly following the latest styles and trying to be like everyone else. I'll see to it that the days of us earthlings acting like a bunch of sheep are over. And I also promise you that from now on I will resist the influence of any aliens who would dare to—"

"You know what, Tina?" said Vikki, very softly and sincerely. "You need to be strong to resist evil alien influences. You'd be *much* stronger at it if you'd lose just a teensy bit of weight. It would make you stronger."

"And cuter," Myndi chirped.

"And *much* more popular," Romi promised. "You can't resist evil alien influences if you don't have enough friends."

"And we'll *help* you do it," Steffi offered with a great big smile. "We've got diet books and exercise videos and—"

"It's *good* for you to be thinner than you are," Lynda said, putting one arm around my shoulders as the five of them led me away.

"Um . . . how much thinner?" I asked.

They all laughed. "Oh, Tina!" Vikki exclaimed. "You can never be *too* thin."

I guess they're right. I mean, it must be true because it's something that everyone knows.

Everyone.

Right?

SCONCE

by Carol Ottolenghi-Barga

B oy, we were lucky to win that game," Kyla said.

"No kidding." Maria flipped her ponytail back as the two girls hurried home from the Kilbourne Junior High soccer match, their green-and-gold soccer bags bouncing against their shoulders and their muddy cleats clattering on the sidewalk. "The referee was against me the whole game. Why should I get carded just because that girl slipped? It wasn't fair."

"It was only a yellow card," Kyla said and grinned. "She sure stayed away from you after you knocked her into the mud."

"She pushed just as hard as I did," Maria said, "but did the ref card *her*? Noooo."

"Well, we won," said Kyla. She shifted her bag to her left shoulder. "I've got to finish my art project tonight. What's *your* project, anyway? You've never said."

"I haven't exactly started it," Maria said.

Kyla sucked in her breath. "You haven't started! Maria—the project's due tomorrow!"

Maria shrugged and bent over to roll her socks down below her shin guards. "I'll think of something. Anyway, it's not really my fault. I had to baby-sit, so I couldn't stay after school and—*Eeuuw!*"

Maria straightened up fast and grabbed Kyla's arm. "Look. Under there." She pointed to a short, wide bush about ten feet in front of them. "That gray blob moved."

Kyla's freckled nose wrinkled in disgust. "What is it? Are you sure it moved?"

"I can't tell." Maria squinted her dark brown eyes and peered harder. "It could be a sick squirrel."

She stepped tiny baby steps toward the bush, holding her soccer bag before her like a shield. When she realized the gray-green blob wasn't going to attack, she knelt and pulled a branch aside for a better view.

It was about a foot high, with shiny, lumpy sides that shimmered in and out rhythmically.

"It's breathing!" Maria cried.

Kyla squatted next to Maria.

"Too weird!" She made a prune face and added, "You're not going to touch it, are you?"

"No way!" Maria's ponytail whipped back and forth when she shook her head. "It looks like a giant booger!"

"I'm supposed to look like a rock," whined a high-pitched voice. "A piece of gray granite, to be exact."

Maria gasped and let go of the branch. The branch smacked Kyla in the face so hard she fell onto her butt. She scrambled to her feet.

"That hurt!" Kyla said angrily as she and Maria huddled on the sidewalk, away from the bush.

"It wasn't my fault," Maria said. "That—that thing made me do it."

"How did you know I wasn't a rock?" demanded the blob. Huffs of irritation made ripples along its sides. "Someone told you, didn't they?"

The girls looked at each other, eyes wide and mouths

hanging open. They took two steps nearer the bush, close enough to see the blob and far enough away to get a really good headstart running if it jumped at them.

"It talks," said Kyla. Her eyes got even wider. "Maria, it talks."

"I can hear that," said Maria, "but what is it?"

"I'm Sconce," the blob said. "A shapeshifter from Blitmore."

Kyla suddenly snapped her fingers and laughed. "I bet it's a puppet," she said. "Someone's playing a trick on us."

"Puppets don't talk by themselves," Maria said, still peering at the blob.

"Maybe it's got one of those electric eyes so that when someone gets close, it starts talking," Kyla said. She picked some mud off her shorts. "You know, like rides at Disney World or the automatic doors at the grocery store."

"Yeah," Maria said. She edged closer to the blob. "Then there's got to be wires or a tape recorder around here somewhere."

She lunged and grabbed the blob. Her finger sunk deep into its sides.

"Let go!" it cried.

The blob wriggled and twisted, but the girl held on tight. Then, without warning, it spat sticky yellow-orange ooze all over Maria's hands.

"Oh, double *eeuuw!*" she screamed. She dropped the blob and wiped her hands wildly against her shirt. "You didn't have to do that!" she yelled. "It is so gross!"

"You didn't have to grab me," the blob said huffily. "It's not my fault I smeared you."

Maria plucked a leaf from the bush and wiped more yellow-orange goo from her hands. "There aren't any wires," she told Kyla.

"Then what is it?" Kyla asked.

"I already told you," the blob said. "I'm Sconce, a shapeshifter from Blitmore."

The girls glanced at each other and then back at Sconce. Maria grabbed Kyla's arm.

"Maybe it's telling the truth," she whispered in Kyla's ear. "Maybe it's an alien!"

"Yeah, right," Kyla said. "There's no—oh, *yuck!* You got that stuff all over me!" She pushed Maria away. "Whoever heard of planet Blitmore?" she asked as she scrubbed her arm with her shirt. "And why would it come here? And"—Kyla stopped scrubbing and put both hands on her hips skeptically—"how does it know English?"

Sconce's sides shimmered in and out. "I've studied your language, geography, sciences and customs for three years. Ever since I graduated to second school."

"So, why are you here?" Maria asked.

Sconce mumbled something, but the girls didn't catch it.

"What?" they asked together.

"Because otherwise I'll flunk," Sconce muttered louder. "It's not my fault," it added quickly. "My teacher hates me. I have to do a research project on human kids to make up for the homework I missed. I thought if I watched some human kids and reported what they did, it would be such a great project that my teacher would have to pass me."

Maria looked around at the bush and sidewalk. "This is a lousy place to choose," she said. "Why didn't you just change into a kid?"

"It's not that easy," Sconce whined, his sides rippling again. "I'm only a foot high, so I can only make shapes that are a foot high. You'd notice a kid that short. I didn't think you'd notice a rock." Sconce sighed. "But you did, and now I'm going to flunk and everyone will laugh at me."

"Maybe not," Maria said. She crossed her arms, put her chin in her right hand, and thought a moment. A slow grin spread over the bottom half of her face and she waggled her eyebrows at Kyla.

"Sconce," Maria said slowly, "watching kids would be a lot easier in school. If you pretended to be my art project, no one would even know you were there."

Kyla's mouth dropped open. "Art project?" she squeaked.

Maria nodded, still grinning.

Kyla put her hand on Maria's shoulder and looked into her face. "Maria," she said very slowly and clearly, "tell me you're not thinking of having a giant booger as your art project."

"A shapeshifter could make a pretty good instant art project," Maria said excitedly. "And we can't let it flunk. This way we both get our projects done." She looked at Sconce. "You *will* make a pretty good art project, won't you?"

"Pretty good?" Sconce puffed himself an inch and a half taller. "I'll make a *great* art project!"

"Then it's settled," Maria said. "You can ride home in my soccer bag."

Kyla hopped back and held her nose. Maria opened her bag. A brown-colored wave of odor rolled out of it—a pungent mix of sweaty socks, forgotten yogurt, and rotten apples.

"Ooof!" Sconce shuddered and flowed backward like a giant slug. "Do I have to?"

Maria scowled. "You have a better way to sneak into my room without my parents knowing? And besides—" her scowl deepened "—it's not *that* bad."

"Oh, noooooo," Kyla said, trying to hold her nose and laugh at the same time.

Ignoring her, Maria put her bag on the ground and opened it wide. Sconce moaned but flowed into it.

"Don't you dare zip this shut," he muttered. "This smell could kill a bliven."

Sconce continued muttering and moaning all the way to Maria's apartment. When they got there, the girls yelled hello to Maria's mom, then rushed the bag into Maria's room and slammed the door. They collapsed on the bed, giggling wildly.

"I can't believe you're doing this," Kyla gasped.

"It'll work," Maria whispered. "You'll see."

"Well, good luck," Kyla said. "See you tomorrow."

After Kyla left, Maria poured Sconce onto her green carpet. She watched, wide-eyed, as Sconce shimmered and changed shape, turning himself inside-outside-upside-rightside-underside. Eight red, leaf-shaped arms sprouted from a supple, trunk-like body. He looked like a very short, very crabby palm tree with a brown snout and two rows of worried eyes.

"Ooooof," he said and wrinkled his snout. "That bag smells worse than the inside of a crogdite's mouth. When do I eat?"

"Eat?" Maria repeated, still staring.

"Yes, eat!" Sconce waved his leaf-arms angrily. "You don't want me to starve to death, do you? Some cool, thick, clammy clay would be delicious, but fresh potting soil will do, if you don't have anything else. And some water, not too cold."

"Not too cold," Maria repeated slowly. She shook her head to clear it, then demanded, "Are you a plant?"

"Not exactly," Sconce said after thinking about it for a moment, "but kind of. Now, about food?"

Maria dumped her wastebasket and carried it into the living room. She scooped two handfuls of soil into it from each of the three plants hanging in the front window. Then she got a bowl of water from the kitchen and returned to her room.

Sconce sniffed hungrily when she put the wastebasket in front of him.

"Ah," he said. His trunk split up the middle into two legs. He lifted them high over the basket's edge, first one and then the other, and burrowed them into the dirt.

"Ah," he said again. "Now pour the water over me."

He gurgled with delight, then started sucking up the dirt like a vacuum cleaner. Maria watched openmouthed until all the dirt was gone. Sconce belched and folded all eight arms over his middle.

"Too weird," Maria said with another shake of her head. She bent to untie her cleats. "Is that your real shape?"

Sconce bent at the middle and belched again. "Yes."

"Well," Maria said, "I think you'll make a great art project just as you are." She started to take off her shirt. "I have to go take a shower. I'll be back— Hey, wait a minute. Are you a boy or girl?"

"I'm a male, if that's what you mean," Sconce said.

"That's *exactly* what I mean," Maria said. "Turn around. I'm not getting undressed in front of a boy."

"What?" Sconce began waving his arms wildly. "It's not *my* fault I'm male! I couldn't care less about your getting undressed—"

Maria stuck him in the closet and shut the door. Sconce huffed and puffed and muttered and sputtered. He was still muttering when Maria came back from her shower and took him out of the closet. He was still muttering when she left the room for dinner. And he was still muttering when she went to bed.

He stopped when she knocked him over with her pillow.

Neither of them was in a great mood the next morning.

"Oh, great," Sconce said when Maria stuck him in her locker. "Oh joy, oh whoop-de-doo. I get to spend the day in your locker."

"*Shhh!*" Maria said and plopped him into the bowl of dirt she'd brought from home. "You're an art project, remember? Art projects don't talk!"

She dumped some ice-cold water from the drinking fountain on him. Sconce sputtered and shivered.

"I can't help that it's cold," Maria whispered and slammed the locker shut.

Kyla pulled her aside in the hall outside their math class.

"How is it?" Kyla whispered.

"It's a *he*," Maria whispered back as they walked into class, "and he's a big pain."

The girls checked on Sconce at lunch.

"I'm hungry," he said. "And I'm bored. I can't do research stuck in a locker."

"I'll get you some dirt," Maria promised and shut the locker again.

"And some water!" he cried out as the girls hurried down the hall. "Warm water!"

The girls' next-to-last period was art. The class set up their projects on the back six tables in the room, next to the sinks. Maria set Sconce next to Kyla's sculpture.

"Where's my dirt?" Sconce whined.

"I'll get it," Maria whispered crabbily. "Now shut up!"

Maria looked at Kyla's sculpture.

"Oooo," she said. "That's really good."

Kyla blushed and pinched her statue's wet, cool clay. It was a dog, a terrier like Kyla's dog, Wow-bow. Swirls of clay curled like wiry fur and the ears perked up like Wow-bow's did when he heard the word "walk."

"Thanks," Kyla said. "I just finished it last night and it's still soft, so I have to be careful. I'm giving it to Dad for Father's Day."

Ms. Olsen, the art teacher, stopped to make title

cards for the girls' projects. "Very creative, Maria," she said, pointing to Sconce. "What's the title?"

" 'Sconce,' " Maria said. She glanced at Kyla, who was looking very hard at the table with her lips squeezed tight, and added, "From Planet Blitmore."

Kyla snorted through her nose, but managed to turn it into a cough.

Ms. Olsen printed out the title card in block letters and put it in front of Sconce. She turned to Kyla's sculpture. Sconce scurried in front of his card to read it.

"Lovely," Ms. Olsen told Kyla. Kyla blushed again. "I can fire it in the kiln for you, if you like. What's your title?"

As she began printing Kyla's title card, she caught sight of Sconce.

"Did you move him?" she asked Maria.

"Ah, y-yes," Maria stammered. "I—I thought it would look funnier if he was pretending to read the card."

"Oh." Ms. Olsen nodded and moved to the next table.

Maria glanced around to see if anyone was watching. No one was except Kyla, so she plucked Sconce up by his trunk.

"You're supposed to stay still," she hissed.

"I'm *hungry*," Sconce whined. "You promised—"

He stopped short when he saw Kyla's clay statue.

"I'll bring you something to eat after last period," Maria said. "But you can't move around. Okay?"

"Okay," Sconce repeated.

Maria didn't notice that only one of Sconce's rows of eyes was looking at her.

The other row was fixed on Kyla's statue.

*   *   *

They had soccer practice after school. On the way home, Maria remembered that she had forgotten to feed and water Sconce.

"One night won't kill him," she told Kyla with a frown. "And it's his own fault, anyway. If he hadn't moved and made me so mad, I wouldn't have forgotten."

Still, when Maria sat down to dinner that night, she thought about Sconce not having anything to eat. She felt a little guilty and promised herself that she'd feed him first thing in the morning.

She got to school early. Avoiding teachers who might ask embarrassing questions, Maria sneaked into the art room with a big bowl of dirt and a water bottle full of warm water. She saw Sconce standing straight up, his eyes closed and his arms folded over his middle.

"Sconce," she said, a little worried that he might be really sick. Or mad. Or both. "Sconce, I brought some dirt and water."

Sconce opened one row of eyes and sniffed.

"Plain dirt," he said, ruffling his snout in disgust. "No, thank you. I've had some of the most delicious clay. I will take some water, though. Being an art project is thirsty work." He held four of his hands out for the water bottle, but Maria ignored them.

"Clay?" she said.

Maria looked at the spot next to Sconce, the spot where Kyla's project had been. She gasped, then picked up Sconce and shook him.

"*Where's Kyla's dog?*" she screamed.

"Quit shaking me!" Sconce huffed and slapped his leaf-like hands against Maria's arms. It didn't hurt, but she quit shaking him. "I *ate* it, of course. After all, you didn't feed me."

"But that doesn't give you the right to eat her statue! She wanted to give it to her dad! Oh, she's going to spaz totally. How *could* you!"

"I can hear you all the way down the hall," Kyla said from the doorway. She walked into the room. "I figured you'd be here early to feed Sconce and I wanted to watch, so I— Hey, where's my dog?"

Maria glared at Sconce. She put him down and then put her arm around Kyla's shoulders.

"I don't know how to tell you this," she began, "but Sconce ate him."

"He *what?*"

Kyla pushed Maria away. She looked under the table, then at the other tables in the room.

"You ate my statue?" Kyla stood over Sconce, fat tears pooling in her eyes, ready to spill over. "Why? I didn't do anything to you."

"I was hungry," Sconce whined. "And it was such beautiful clay."

Kyla whirled on Maria. "He was hungry because *you* didn't feed him!" she yelled.

"*He* ate it!" Maria yelled back. "It's not *my* fault!"

"It's *never* your fault, is it?" Kyla's lips trembled, and the tears were spilling down her cheeks, but she went right on talking. "When you foul someone in soccer, it's not your fault. When you forget your homework, it's not your fault. When you don't feed your—your Sconce, and he eats my sculpture, it's not your fault."

Kyla wiped the back of her hand across her face and continued. "Well, guess what, Maria—it *is* your fault! It's your fault when you foul someone, and it's your fault when you forget your homework, and it's your fault that Sconce ate my statue!"

"Kyla—"

"Don't talk to me!" Kyla cried. "Don't *ever* talk to me again. I can't believe I thought you were my best friend!"

She ran out of the room. Maria heard the door of the girls restroom across the hall squeak open, then bang shut.

Maria and Sconce were silent for a long moment. Finally, Sconce said, "She seemed a little upset."

"She's *very* upset," Maria said. She sniffed and two tears rolled down her right cheek. "She worked hard on that statue."

Maria sighed. "It's—it's *my* fault that you ate it," she told Sconce. "I have to tell her I'm sorry. I can't give her back her statue, but at least I can tell her it was my fault." She sniffed again. "Maybe she'll forgive me. Or maybe not for a long time."

She lifted up Sconce until she could look into both his rows of eyes. "And I'm sorry I didn't feed you," she said. "I should have remembered. Then you wouldn't have been hungry and Kyla would still have her statue."

Sconce's arms were folded around his trunk and his snout was blue and wrinkled. He honked and Maria guessed he was crying. Or something.

"I didn't mean to upset her," he said and honked

again. "Maybe I *shouldn't* have eaten it." He honked a third time, then said timidly, "I'll understand if you don't want to help me with my project anymore."

"No, I'll still help you," Maria said. She put Sconce back down, then smiled a crooked smile. "Maybe you can research how humans say I'm sorry," she added. "I'm not very good at that."

"That's a great idea!" Sconce rustled his leaf-arms over his snout and eyes. "If I disguise myself as a notebook, I can lie around the halls and—"

"Tell me later," Maria said. "Right now, I have to apologize."

She walked into the hall and headed toward the girls restroom to find Kyla.

CHILDHOOD'S CONFESSION

by Lou Grinzo

My name is Hank Innes, and I'm writing this to correct the public's view of the Visitor Fight. It's been over forty years since it happened, and, except for the official version, there's hardly been a single word printed or publicly said about it since Richard Polanski's trial. Because of this, everyone still thinks of Polanski as the lowlife he was portrayed to be. This is inaccurate and unfair, and it should be corrected.

To date, no one has been able to tell what really happened the day of the fight, the day the Visitors left Earth in disgust and headed back to their planet, wherever that is. None of us who were involved wanted to challenge the government and try to get our account of it published, even anonymously. That's why you'll be reading this such a long time after the Visitor Fight, after I'm dead, when even the government can't do anything to me.

Where to begin? The popular view of what happened that day is full of the reckless nature of Richard Polanski and the innocent behavior of ten-year-old boys. Both parts are just plain wrong. Polanski, God rest his soul, was a decorated Army officer with an outstanding service record, and he was a well-respected member of the Secret Service. But he made a bad decision under the kind of pressure that would destroy most people.

As for the childrens' part in what happened, I know

better than anyone why the fight really happened. You see, it was my fault.

For most people, the terrible events of that day are recorded in that single black-and-white newspaper photograph. Sure, there are the tapes of the trial and the interviews and the live TV reports from the site, but the event collapses into that one photograph, showing a group of small boys standing around a body on the ground.

It's funny how that happens, how a shutter tripped by a photographer's instinct creates an image that instantly becomes *the* photograph that tells a story, as if all of mankind had conferred and agreed on the matter. It happens all the time, of course, but that doesn't make it any easier to understand. That one portrait of Princess Diana that's been the unofficial portrait of her ever since she died. The photograph of TWA Flight 800 wreckage floating in the water. Michael Jordan hugging the NBA championship trophy. The Visitor Fight. Each historic moment, compressed forever into a single negative.

It's important that you understand what it was like, being in the fourth grade and having an honest-to-goodness *alien* in your class. You've seen the pictures of the Visitors. How they didn't wind up being tagged with some stupid name straight out of a bad science-fiction movie, I'll never know. The point is, from the day "Bob" showed up at school, life ceased to be normal.

One day, a group of men in suits walked into our classroom—right in the middle of a history lesson, I can still remember it that clearly, we were learning about Shay's

Rebellion—and the look on our teacher's face instantly told us something unusual was happening. One of the men was the President of the United States. Most of the rest were probably Secret Service agents, although I didn't know that at the time. There was a White House photographer and a single TV news team there to record the exact moment when an alien child entered a human classroom. The class was dead silent as we tried to understand what was going on. Keep in mind that the public had only seen the Visitors on TV up until that point, and even then it was mostly staged photo opportunities with world leaders.

The alien kid and one of his parents came shuffling in. He was taller than all the kids in the room, dressed in one of those silky blue robes they wore, all horrid looking and wheezing, with too many arms, and breathing some sort of gas mixture through a respirator connected to a lunch box–sized contraption he carried. The class erupted. It should have been clear to the adults involved that this was a bad idea, and they should have found a diplomatic way to call it off right then and there. But they didn't, of course.

Once everything calmed down, the President made his famous "Children of the Universe" speech, which I'm sure you've heard a thousand times, and explained how this Visitor child would attend our school as a sign of mutual trust. Our teacher, a frail little woman with huge, liquid brown eyes, looked like she was going to have a break-down. Even then, I remembered feeling sorry for her.

From that day on, a significant part of our lives was spent avoiding reporters. But the kids got the worst of it.

Every recess, every school function, even the slightest sign that something the least bit out of the ordinary was going on at the school was cause for us to be swarmed by reporters carrying cameras and bright lights and microphones up and down the halls. It took a while before the media and our parents came to an agreement, but there were still intrusions and occasional parental lectures.

We weren't even aware of what the Visitors were doing here. All those meetings that they had at the United Nations, all the hints of wondrous things that could come out of a friendship between our species, none of it was explained to us at the time. The adults were scared stiff that we would do something inconvenient and screw it all up. No one even tried to make us see things from Bob's point of view. He was probably scared out of his mind. Maybe the way they treated us contributed in some small way to what happened.

Bob didn't seem to be bothered by any of it, although it was hard to tell. I guess the pressure on him was even worse than it was for the rest of us, considering how difficult it was for him to communicate with us. Any race that would put one of their children into a position like that would probably have lectured the kid to death on how important it was that he behave himself. But who knows, if this species was that concerned with such things, maybe it's part of their nature, and they wouldn't *have* to stress it.

But I feel like I'm avoiding the issue here.

Thomas Alva Edison grade school, in Union City, New Jersey, is your average inner-city public school. There are lots of fights, and almost every group of boys knows of at least one fight that will take place after school on any given day. But on the day it happened, there were no arranged fights, at least none that were exciting enough for the gang I hung out with. So one of us came up with the idea of getting the class bully, Karl, into a fight with Bob. I was the one; it was my idea.

I won't try to justify what happened with some sort of flippant "boys will be boys" attitude. None of us saw the ramifications of what we were doing. We'd been lectured almost nonstop since Bob came to our school about how important it was that we got along, that we "set an example" for humans and Visitors. God, how I learned to hate that phrase, "set an example." No one let us forget for a minute the strange microscope we were all under. The point of all this is simply that, yes, we were little boys, but we knew better.

It was so easy to start, too. A couple of us simply dared Karl to fight Bob. That, plus a little encouragement, was all it took, since Karl lived for chances to be a tough guy. Several others talked to Bob and somehow convinced him that he had to defend his honor or some such nonsense, not that I think he fully understood what was happening. We were just pleased with having arranged something exciting. Now, I can see how ridiculous and foolish it all was, but at the moment, I was thrilled to have started it.

When school let out that day, about fifteen of us followed Karl and Bob down the block and into the empty lot behind our favorite candy store. There was the usual little boy bravado about it all—everyone was talking tough and taking sides and savoring the delicious anticipation of it, especially *this* fight. Karl dramatically dropped his books and took off his dark blue windbreaker and threw it down. A bunch of us started pushing and moving around for a good view. Bob just stood there, with his skinny, ropy arms at his sides, obviously unaware of what was expected. Karl walked up to him and pushed him hard on one shoulder, and that's when things got crazy.

Cars squealed to a stop in the street; doors opened and men in dark suits came piling out too fast for anyone to react. They all had guns. One man in particular—Richard Polanski—walked toward Karl and Bob. He pointed at them with one hand—the one without the gun—and said, "OK, boys, let's break it up. We don't want to have a fight here."

Those were his exact words. I'll never forget them or the pleading, almost hysterical tone in his voice. It was as if he knew with absolute certainty what was going to happen, and he wanted desperately to stop the future from coming true.

Karl got this defiant look on his face, that same look he'd get every time he was about to do something to anger a teacher. He turned away, as if to comply with Polanski's request, then turned back around and punched Bob in the face. The alien teetered for a second, then hit the ground flat on his back.

And Polanski shot Karl. A single, clean shot in the chest that threw him to the ground, dead.

One of the other men started screaming, "What did you do that for? Where are your brains? Give me your gun, Polanski!"

Some of us started crying, some of us just stood and stared at Karl on the ground, and a couple of us turned and ran home. I was convinced that these men with guns—Secret Service agents, I found out later—knew about my part in the fight and were going to shoot me as punishment. I kept looking breathlessly at each one in turn, trying to spot the one who would do it, waiting for one of them to raise his gun.

Reporters and the local police were there in minutes, and that's when the famous picture was taken. I'm the second kid from the left in the crowd, the terrified one wearing the white polo shirt and dark pants.

The archived news reports say that somehow all the Visitors knew at that moment what had happened, and they turned to whomever they were with and demanded to be brought together, and to see Bob. As soon as the delegation was assembled and they determined that Bob was not seriously hurt, they had a brief meeting and gave the highest ranking person available, Secretary of State Frankel, their famous message: We refuse to associate with barbarians.

Within days of the shooting, Richard Polanski was the victim of the biggest smear campaign in the history of mankind. He was a decent man who made a mistake, but everyone ganged up on him—the media, the government, old friends. He was branded a maverick, a "loose cannon" who refused to follow orders—everything they could hang on him to "prove" to the Visitors that Polanski wasn't a fair example of what mankind was really like. No one had the guts to stand up and say, "Wait a minute. Dick was a good man who messed up. Let's have a little compassion here." We were pleading to the sky, screaming for the Visitors to come back, and Richard Polanski was sacrificed in the process.

For a case with that kind of pretrial publicity, it should have taken weeks, or even months, to pick a jury. But they did it in a single day. It took an emergency session of the New Jersey state legislature to legalize capital punishment, but they did that in record time, too.

The trial itself was a farce, as one liar after another was paraded through the witness stand. One piece of falsified evidence after another was presented. And all of it was choreographed to say exactly the right things, while Polanski's defense was a fraud. And when the two-day trial was over, they pronounced him guilty of first degree murder and sentenced him to death in the electric chair.

But the worst part was the execution. They showed it on television! The rationale was obvious. They wanted to make absolutely sure that the Visitors knew what we did. But didn't anyone in charge have the brains to see what a mistake it was? If the aliens had had any thought of coming back, that surely drove them away for good.

About twenty years after his death, I talked to Nicole Polanski, Richard's widow. She was in her late fifties by then, but she looked much older. Her hair was almost completely gray, and the lines around her granite-colored eyes showed the burden she'd lived with. It was as if her ordeal had never ended, and had continuously worn her down over the years. We took great pains to be clandestine, although I doubt we fooled anyone. If the CIA or anyone else still cared, they probably knew what we were doing but figured we were harmless.

Nicole insisted that I watch recordings of the trial with her, so she could refute the lies one at a time. It was like a private trial, decades after her husband's death, as she clutched at a chance to prove to someone that her husband wasn't an ogre. The way she swiftly and confidently argued against the images on the screen, it was clear to me that she'd rehearsed this a hundred times, waiting for an audience. In all those years, no one was willing to publish her story or a single interview with her.

If the law firm I hired does their job, and the government doesn't intervene, then this document will be sent to every major newspaper and radio and TV station in the civilized world. The fact that I got this far with my arrangements gives me hope that this account will get published. Maybe everyone's finally given up trying to lure the Visitors back, and the government's realized it's time to drop the public act.

Just as my friends and I were children that day, and we didn't understand what we were doing, the entire human race unwittingly proved that it was still in its own childhood, not yet fit to associate with the adults as an equal partner.

Hank Innes
Wilkes-Barre, PA
17 November 2041

VERY SMART

by Marc Bilgrey

Being smart doesn't solve all your problems, at least not usually. Take me, for instance. My name's Robert Sutton, I'm twelve years old, and I'm a genius. Well, I don't feel like a genius, but that's what the test said I was. Mom and Dad took me to some office where they asked me all kinds of questions and had me play with blocks and other stuff and then, a couple of weeks later, the results came back: genius.

Since Mom and Dad found out about it, it's the only thing they talk about. They talk about it with their friends, the neighbors, and on the phone with relatives I haven't even met. All I know is I still have to eat my vegetables, I still have to clean my room, and I still have to go to school. So I guess it hasn't really changed anything, except every so often Dad will say, "Hey, why are you watching TV? Geniuses don't watch TV." Well, since I like to watch TV, I guess geniuses *do* watch TV.

Anyway, like I said, since finding out about how smart I am, everything's exactly the same, and, I guess, that's the problem. Let me explain that. See, there's this kid in my math class, Jimmy Fenner, and every day after school he waits for me, beats me up, and steals my allowance. Sometimes I manage to run home before he can grab me, but usually he catches me. This has been going on for months. In fact, I don't like to admit it, but it's made me scared to go out. All I think about every day is Jimmy Fenner waiting for me.

I've thought about telling Mom and Dad about it, but I know that they'll just say what they've been saying about everything lately, which is, "Geniuses don't get into fights." Every time I do something they don't like, they always say, "Geniuses don't—whatever." The other thing I'm worried about is that if my dad ever did find out he'd call up Jimmy's dad and then word would get out and everyone would think that I'm a chicken who can't fight his own battles.

So, I'm stuck. I even bought a book on karate, but being smart doesn't make you coordinated. I tried to work out some of the moves from the book and fell down on the floor in my room.

The other thing that bothers me about this whole Jimmy Fenner situation is that the other kids in my class all know about it. How could they not? It happens in front of the school just about every day. A lot of the kids have been making fun of me about it. They'll say stuff like, "Going out for a little run, Robert?" Or, "Hey, Robert, I hear Jimmy wants to use his punching bag later."

One day, I managed to sneak out the school's back door and avoid Jimmy. Instead of going home, I just kept walking. In fact, I walked all the way out of town. The whole time I was turning around, ready to run if I had to. Luckily, I didn't have to. So, I just kept walking. After a while, I managed to stop thinking about Jimmy and thought about plans for a couple of inventions I was working on. I'm always trying to come up with something—maybe that's why my grades aren't better. The things I work on are usually a lot more interesting than my school assignments, and I guess I spend more time on them than I should. "Geniuses should do their homework," my dad is always saying.

I walked for a while longer till I came to a big, open field, a couple of miles from town. By now it was getting dark. I sat down on the grass and took out my notepad and wrote down some ideas for a bird-feeding machine I'd come up with. Then I heard this strange humming sound. I turned around, trying to figure out where it was coming from, when I looked up and saw this bright light moving across the sky.

The light got closer and then I saw it was a saucer-shaped spaceship! Seriously! I jumped up and watched it hover above me. It was maybe fifty feet wide. Suddenly, a light went on under it and then someone appeared in front of me. He was wearing a tight silver suit. He had green skin like a lizard and yellow eyes.

"Wow!" I said.

"You are Robert Sutton?" said the alien.

"Yeah, but how'd you know that?" I said.

"We've been studying your planet and you in particular."

"Why've you been studying me?" I was scared but also kind of excited.

"Excuse me, I do not know all your customs. I have been rude. Allow me to introduce myself first. I am Klarzak, from the planet Ronor."

"Pleased to meet you," I said, remembering what my

dad always told me I should say when I got introduced to someone.

Instead of shaking my hand, he just held his up. I imitated him.

"Now then," said Klarzak, "as to why we have been studying you. We have been collecting the most brilliant beings of all the inhabited planets in the galaxy, to take them to a special world where they will try to solve the problems of the universe."

"Oh?" I said, not exactly following what he was getting at.

"Don't you see?" said Klarzak. "You are the most intelligent being on your planet."

"Well, I know I got a high score on that test but—"

"We want to take you to be with others of your intelligence level."

"How long will I be away?" I asked.

"Many of your years," said the alien. "Perhaps all of your life."

"What exactly would I be doing on this special planet? What kinds of problems would I be trying to solve?"

"Wars, disease, everything that has plagued the inhabited worlds," said Klarzak.

"You're going to kidnap me?" I said, feeling more than a little scared now.

"No, you will go of your own free will."

"What if I don't want to?"

"That is your right. We will give you twenty-four of your hours to make your decision. If you decide to go, come back to this location tomorrow. If not, I would appreciate you returning here to explain your reason or reasons for not accompanying us. Now go and think it over."

With that, Klarzak vanished, and then the spaceship zipped off faster than anything I'd ever seen before.

When I got home, Mom and Dad were annoyed that I was late, but when I told them that I was working on a science project in the woods they quieted down. After dinner, I went up to my room and thought about the alien's offer. I've always loved science-fiction novels and I've seen just about every movie with a starship in it, but this was different. The idea of actually being able to go to another planet, for real was hard to imagine. And to do something to help other people and other civilizations, that was beyond amazing.

As I sat in my room looking out at the night sky, I suddenly thought about Jimmy Fenner. If I was on another planet I'd never have to get beaten up by him again. That sounded great! I'd never have to worry about leaving school hoping that Jimmy wouldn't get me. I wouldn't miss that. And I wouldn't miss school either, come to think of it. I certainly wouldn't miss doing homework. Or cleaning my room.

I went to my closet and took out my travel bag. I threw a few pairs of underwear and socks and a couple of shirts into the bag. Then I put in my toothbrush and a new tube of toothpaste. Klarzak hadn't told me what to bring, but I figured that they would have clothes where I was going.

The next day, I went to school as if it was just another day. After each period I thought about the fact that this would

be the last time that I would ever be in English, social studies or math again. Math. That's when I saw Jimmy Fenner.
He gave me that look he always gives me. The "I'll be seeing you later" look. *Ha,* I thought. *Those days are over, too.*

When the last bell rang, I sprinted out of school
through the back door, and then something made me
walk toward the front of the building. I peered around
the corner and saw Jimmy leaning against a car.

At that moment, I thought about Mom and Dad and
warm summer nights and comic books and videotapes of
old TV shows and pizza. And then I slowly walked out
from behind the building. Jimmy saw me immediately and
began coming toward me. That's when I started running. I
ran like I've never run before, and all the while Jimmy
Fenner was right behind me. In a few minutes we were out
of town. And after that, we were in the open field and then,
just as Jimmy Fenner was gaining on me, the flying saucer
showed up. Jimmy stopped in his tracks and stared at it.

A few seconds later, Klarzak appeared in front of me.
"Robert Sutton," said Klarzak, "what is your decision?"

"Klarzak," I said, "you're looking for the most intelligent being on this planet to represent the Earth on this
special planet you're going to. Yesterday you said it was
me. Well, you were wrong."

"What?" said Klarzak. "But we have been studying
you—"

"That's right, you have, but doesn't it stand to reason
that the most intelligent being on this planet would hide
that fact so as not to be bothered? Klarzak, I'd like you to
meet the most intelligent being on Earth: Jimmy Fenner."

Klarzak looked at Jimmy, who was standing about fifteen feet from us, frozen like a deer in car headlights. "Are you sure that this—" Klarzak began to say.

"Yes, I'm positive," I said, "but he's a little shy. Anyway, I've told him everything you've said and, though you can't tell by looking at him, he's very anxious to go with you and solve problems."

Klarzak stared at me and Jimmy. Then Klarzak disappeared into his spaceship and, a few seconds later, Jimmy vanished, too. After that, the ship zoomed off into the night.

I stood looking at the stars and thought about how good I felt. Usually on a weeknight I was sad or worried. Then the strangest thing of all happened. I started thinking about going to school in the morning and realized that, for the first time in months, I was actually looking forward to it. Laughing to myself, I turned around and started walking home.

"How's your science project coming?" asked my dad after I showed up late again and sat down to dinner.

"It's coming along really well," I said, digging into my vegetables.

"You seem very happy today," said Mom.

"Oh, I am," I replied.

"Any particular reason?" she asked.

"Did you ever have one of those days where everything seemed to go right?" I said.

FINDING THE WAY

by Sherwood Smith

*H*onk! Honk!

The damage alarm was louder than the pings and klonks of the meteorite shower our scout ship had accidentally encountered on our emergence from hyperspace.

"A puncture! We're losing energy!" Kikinee shrilled.

"Teer! Noot! Take evasive action," the Vmmm's voice hummed over the intercom. "I will fix the puncture."

Teer waved at me to take piloting as she worked at her computer. I did my best to guide our scout ship around the biggest meteorites. There was no time to set up a course. I punched us back into hyperdrive, and the screens smeared as our engines took us between dimensions.

With no idea where we were going, I yelled to our navigator, "Thisko, can't you—"

"Navigational computer is down," Thisko said, five of his eight tentacles working away.

"At least if we drop out of hyper into a planet," came Smelch's mournful hoot, "we won't have to spend five long hours in the Room for Reviewing Actions."

Kikinee waved at a cable that had shaken loose when the first big rock hit the ship, and chirped, "Quiet, Smelch, and give me a hand with that gravity-link."

Still muttering, Smelch shot one of its six hands across the cabin to the danging wires. The fingers quickly maneuvered the gravity-link back to where it ought to be, and we felt gravity ripple through the ship again.

Then Kikinee tossed the hand back across the cabin and, with a loud *splorch!*, it reattached to Smelch's arm.

We were all strapped into our pods, so we hadn't floated, but a couple of the things that had come loose—like part of Kikinee's lunch—stopped floating and dropped with a *thud, klank*, and a squashy noise. Kikinee and Smelch scrambled to clean up. When things were stable again, I pulled us back into the real-time dimension, hoping we would emerge in the safety of space.

We were lucky.

"We're near a system," Thisko said after a pause, and sent the coordinates to my screen. "Noot, get us there. The third planet shows that the atmosphere is mainly oxygen and nitrogen—"

"Is the planet on the survey list?" came the Vmmm's voice. "Dangerous life-form warnings?"

"Class Five listing for this system," Teer said, checking Thisko's data.

I was still busy piloting us toward the mysterious planet, and trying to shed the enormous velocity built up during our jump between dimensions.

"Average sun, ten planets in all . . . looks like one broke up . . ." Teer went on.

The scout ship bucked again.

"No details now," I said. "We're still not stable! I'm taking us to the planet with the oxygen. At least we can breathe that."

Except for the Vmmm, of course—but the Vmmm

doesn't need to breathe. A capsule of carbon dioxide once a lunar orbit, and the Vmmm is fine.

"Third planet in from the primary . . ." Teer said, scanning. "Noot! Slow us down! We're approaching way too fast! We'll bounce off the atmosphere and back into space!"

"I'm trying," I yelped, braking us hard. Energy was disappearing fast.

I used the atmosphere itself as a brake, looping tightly around the planet twice. When our speed was not going to cause us to burn up on entering the planet's atmosphere, I dropped us toward the planet, this time using the atmosphere to help brake us despite how hot it made the outside of the scout ship. We had very little energy left—just enough to land us.

I cut in the thrusters at the last possible moment, and once we'd gone aerodynamic, it was time to look for a place to set down.

"Life-form readings," Kikinee chirped. "Lots. Especially in these areas with all the cubes."

"Must be domiciles." The Vmmm's voicebox vibrated warningly. "Avoid those."

"Keep us cloaked until the last moment," Thisko warned. "And keep us high enough to cool off the exterior of the craft!"

"I see a nice space there, past those tall things that look like giant vorch," I said, steering the craft down in a gentle circle. "Right next to the water."

"Trees," Teer said, peering into his viewer. "I have the language converter working. Those tall, rooted things are called trees."

"Shall we talk to them?" Vmmm said.

"I don't trust life-forms that don't move," Smelch added mournfully.

"According to the computer, the life-forms that have audible language have two legs—"

"Like those ones?" Thisko looked down through the viewscreen. "Look at them, running about on the green filaments."

"Grass," Teer said, working quickly. "And the life-forms are the youth of the local sentient species."

"Like us!" I cried.

"Not like us, Noot," Teer said warningly. "They aren't cadet-scouts in the Interplanetary Trade School."

Thisko waved his tentacles. "This is true," he said. "Supposedly these life-forms have not traveled to other worlds—that's what 'Class Five' means!"

No one spoke for a long time. We couldn't imagine what it would be like not to travel to other worlds—not even to know about them.

"Tell us more about these life-forms," Kikinee chirped.

"Well, they come in two kinds," Teer started.

"A perplexing arrangement," Smelch commented sadly. Its world has only one kind of people—after twenty years each citizen has an egg, and that's that for family.

"Boring," Thisko said, his tentacles vibrating. On *his* world, there are five kinds of people, and a young person might change two or three times before deciding whether to be a her, a him, a lon, a ril, or a zee. And when you want to start a family, you have to have all five together—one of each kind. Family life on Thisko's world is very, very complicated.

"The types are called 'boys' and 'girls,'" Teer went on. Teer and I nodded—we have the same on our world. The males stay home in the hive, and we females go out to work.

"Which one is which?" Kikinee whistled, bobbing near the viewscreen. "They all look exactly alike to me."

"It doesn't matter." Smelch sighed. "We don't dare stay long enough to interact with them. We'll be in bogs of trouble as it is."

The Vmmm hummed briskly. "Smelch is right. Let's get what we need and lift again before we really start breaking the Fourteen Laws of Interference."

Before anyone could speak, the ship, which had been zooming along fairly quietly, gave a *bleep*, and a *zoop*, and *thunk!* We landed on the grass not far from the water.

"Our ship's energy is zapped," I said.

"Then *we're* zapped," Smelch moaned.

No one answered.

Because the cloaking device was still working, the young life-forms had not seen us, and for a short time we watched them running about, kicking at a round shape. I was wondering what to do now.

"They really *are* all exactly alike," Teer said. "Look! They all have two legs, two arms, two eyes—"

"One nose," Kikinee offered. "That's at least a *bit* of variety."

"Only if others of them had four noses, or six, or

three," Smelch said, rubbing two of its noses. Growing extra noses is common on its world. They are all enthusiastic about smell-o-vision there.

"They aren't completely alike," Kikinee whistled. "The faces and hands and the filaments atop their heads—"

"Hair," Teer said, looking into the computer.

"Well, the hair seems to be brown and black and yellow and there's a red one. But their fur looks like various shades of brown. Kind of boring, to be mostly the same color. Not a green or a blue in sight."

"Or even a handsome purple—like us," Teer said, pointing at herself and me.

"That's not fur," Vmmm said. "That's a kind of flimsy carapace—not solid like yours."

"It's not a carapace," Kikinee put in. "It's a little like feathers—"

"It's skin," Teer corrected, looking into the computer. "And the cloth is called 'clothing' . . . no, it's called 'bathing suits.'"

Everyone spoke at once. "What's that?"

"Decorative protection," Teer reported, tapping at the computer pads.

"Weird," Kikinee hooted.

"Embarrassing," Thisko pronounced. "I would not like to have to wear strangely-colored plant fibers over my pelt. What if you can't get your tentacles free when you need them?"

"These beings don't have tentacles," Smelch said sadly.

"Poor things," Thisko said, but softly. Rule One of

the Nine Rules of Polite Interaction is not to brag about your race's attributes—and Rule Two is not to comment about another being's lack.

"Only one nose," Smelch grumbled, breaking Rule Two again.

No one said anything—we were all too shaken up by our close call.

"We must plan." The Vmmm's voice hummed like a hive of stickle-insects, a sure sign zir was upset. It's not safe to get the Vmmm upset.

Everyone was quiet for a moment.

I said, "Our first need is energy."

Thisko said, "Scanning for sources . . . ah. Next to the water. This light brown stuff is full of it. We'll have to filter—"

"That's sand," Teer said.

On our world, we have lots of sand, but it's not brown, it's purple—like us. Thisko's world is all ice, and they live in towers.

"What if it's valuable?" Kikinee chirped. "We ought not just to take it. Then we are breaking the First Rule of Equitable Trade!"

"But we haven't anything to offer in return," Teer said. "We're on a scouting assignment, after all, not a trade assignment."

Silence again.

We turned to the Vmmm.

"We will have to speak with the life-forms," the Vmmm hummed, louder than before.

That hum made us scramble into action.

Thisko decloaked the ship. Teer programmed the computer to translate the local language. Kikinee let down the ramp. We all breathed the air—which smelled of salt and herbs—then Smelch sneezed, and three of its noses flew off, one of them landing outside on the grass.

"Eeeeuw! What's that?" one of the life-forms yelled, pointing at Smelch. The computer translated the language into our headsets.

"Looks like a ball of guts with body parts stuck all over," another said.

"That's Smelch," I said carefully, and the computer's translator took my words and broadcast them in the local language. "It needs to retrieve one of its noses."

"Wow! One of the giant purple lobsters talks English!"

"Extra noses? That's disgusting—" a fourth life-form started, but a tall one, with dark skin and hair, waved a hand and the others stopped talking.

"Not where it comes from, I bet. We might be the disgusting ones."

The other life-forms looked at us quietly. We looked back.

"AyYesha is right," a little one chirped in a voice kind of like Kikinee's. "Me, I think they look kinda cool. All of 'em! Are you guys, like, in a movie or something?"

"Movie," Teer said, tapping her belt computer. "Oh! It's an entertainment form."

"Like smell-o-vision," Smelch said, sounding happy for once.

93

"We need an energy source," I said. "Silicon."

"Sand is full of it," the life-form called AyYesha said.

"We know," Kikinee chirped, fluffing his feathers. "We wish to effect a trade."

"What do you got?" a small life-form asked.

"Just a sec," AyYesha said, stepping forward. "We should introduce ourselves. I'm AyYesha, and here's my little sister NaTasha. She's Laurie, and those boys are Adam, Mick, and Kenji."

AyYesha was a girl, then. Teer said, "We are Teer and Noot. Here's Kikinee, and Thisko, and Smelch. Inside is the Vmmm."

"The what?" Adam asked.

"The Vmmm," I said. "Every ship has one."

"May we look inside?" AyYesha asked.

"Please do," Thisko said, glad that things were starting out like a proper trade ought to.

The boys and girls swarmed inside the ship, curious about everything, some using their arm-digits to touch things. AyYesha moved very slowly, examining everything with close attention.

"Wow, look at that computer," Kenji exclaimed. "I could use one of those!"

"It smells so good in here," NaTasha said to me.

"That's the Vmmm," I told her. "They get CO_2 once a month, and the rest of the time they spurt out pure oxygen. Unless they get angry."

"You mean they fart good air?" Mick asked, making a hooting noise. "Where's this guy hiding?"

"The Vmmm is fixing the energy compartment," I

said. "And zir is not hiding—they just don't come out into the light. It hurts them unless they wear a coating of light-blocking alloy. But zir is listening. The Vmmm always listen."

AyYesha turned from studying our piloting console. "You mean they are telepathic?"

We looked at one another. "The Vmmm seem to hear one another no matter where they are," Thisko said, waving two tentacles. "But I don't know if they hear us when we don't speak."

"So, what shall we trade you for your sand?" Teer asked. "We must get it loaded and converted."

"Your flight tech," AyYesha said quickly.

"This computer," Kenji said almost as fast.

Thisko and Teer said to the rest of us in our Universal Trade Language, *"Remember Class Five!"*

We weren't even supposed to be talking to these beings, much less trading for technology they didn't have.

"Don't tell me," Adam said. "You got these rules, right?"

"How did you know?" I asked. "Have you heard of the Interplanetary Trade School?"

The two biggest, AyYesha and Adam, looked at each other.

Behind, I heard the Vmmm humming.

Kikinee whistled his I-hear-trouble whistle.

"No," AyYesha said at last. "We haven't. We didn't even know that other life exists—some of our scientists don't believe it."

"And won't, even if we try to tell them," Adam

added. "Who believes kids? They'll just turn us over to a counselor."

"Or tell us to stop eating so much junk food," Kenji added in a sour voice.

"Junk? Food?" Smelch's mournful voice interrupted. "Do you consume recyclables? Sounds very efficient."

"Nope," NaTasha said, giggling. "Food that tastes good but doesn't make you grow or anything. Parents hate it——except for the kinds they like to eat."

"Ah, like nid-nuts," Teer said, and I nodded.

"But if we show them some cool kind of new technology, like how this ship works," Mick said, waving his arms, "then they'd have to believe us! And we can get to space sooner!"

"Who says the government won't just sit on it?" Adam said.

"Publish on the Internet," Kenji said, turning to face him. "Then everyone can make a spaceship."

"And what then? Take our wars into space? Gangs staking claim on the moon?" AyYesha said. "Look, guys, we got enough problems on our planet. I think we're going to have to solve them before we get into space, or we'll just have bigger problems and drag all these others into them." She waved at us.

"So what do we trade?" Adam asked, crossing his arms in front of him. "Teer said they have to trade."

"The sand is free for everyone," AyYesha said. "And we got to meet them. We 'trade' something that doesn't belong to us anyway, that belongs to the whole world, for the knowledge that they are here. And maybe, someday, we can give that knowledge to the world. I'd say that's fair."

Adam looked down at his feet. Then he looked up. "Fair," he said.

Behind us, the Vmmm's hum had stopped.

"Here, let's all help them load sand," Laurie said.

We all worked together, scooping sand into our energy converter. It stripped out the silicon and spat out the sand again, which landed back on the shore, slightly lighter in color but otherwise unharmed.

As we worked, Mick gave a quick glance inside our ship, then said to me in a soft voice, "What happens if that Vmmm thing gets mad?"

"Zir emits sulfur instead of oxygen."

"Sulfur farts?" Mick said, making his eyes round and his mouth squeeze up like a molting plip-bug. "Whew! Let's keep this guy happy, definitely."

Behind us, Thisko gave a muffled laugh.

"Done," Teer called, reading her belt computer. "The energy compartment is sealed, and we have plenty of energy."

"We had better go," Kikinee said.

"Cloaking on," Thisko added.

Now only our ramp was visible. The rest of the ship was a blur, reflecting the surroundings. We retreated up the ramp, leaving the boys and girls standing on the sand, watching.

"Good-bye," Adam said.

The little ones all waved. AyYesha now had her arms folded. Her black eyes did not blink as she watched.

"Farewell," I called, and closed the ramp.

Thisko's tentacles worked at the navigation console, and Teer and I sat at the piloting controls. As our ship quietly lifted to a height at which it was safe to fire the thrusters without burning anything below, we all watched the beings dwindling in size until they were invisible against the sand. Then I cut in the thrusters, and we zoomed upward over the great blue expanse of water.

As we rose, the Vmmm's voice came: "A job well done."

Then a sweet infusion of oxygen came wafting through the ship. As we raced into the darkness of space, the stars clear and sharp, the Vmmm added, "AyYesha. We must remember that name. I believe we will see her again."

JILLY

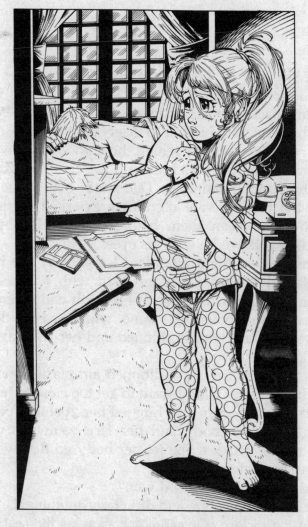

by Deborah Wheeler

The summer he was twelve, Evan's baby sister, Jilly, spent a month with Cousin Edith in Chicago and when she came back, she had changed. Evan's first clue came when he went with his dad to meet her at the little country airport. Evan waited behind the outdoor gate, watching how the wire fences broke up the cloudless Kansas sky into rounded diamonds. Dad strode over to the field where the small private aircraft were parked, staring as if he'd never seen them before. When Jilly's plane landed, he followed it with his eyes.

A redheaded flight attendant led Jilly by the hand. Jilly started toward Evan and Dad with a big smile, showing the gap where one of her teeth had fallen out. Otherwise, she looked the same, with her bony knees that were always getting skinned and her flyaway hair the color of pine wood.

Her hair smelled of conditioned air, plastic, and airplane fumes. Evan didn't want to get too close to her.

Dad picked her up and hugged her. A shiver passed through her thin body and her face went pale right down to her freckles. She let her body go floppy until Dad put her down.

Dad said, "We've missed you."

She looked up at him and didn't say anything. Driving back in the pickup, she sat as far away as the seat belts would allow. Evan decided she must still be airsick. Jilly always had something to say about everything. Now, glancing at her round, unblinking eyes and pinched-in mouth, he wondered if this was the same kid.

Dad pulled up in the graveled front yard. A patch of daisies shimmered in the afternoon heat. The two dogs lay panting under the apple tree by the picket fence, well away from the house. Mom caught Jilly in her arms, then glanced at Dad.

"What's wrong? Is she sick?"

"Must be," he said.

She's just tired, Evan thought, but even then he knew that wasn't it.

Mom said, "Well then, up to bed, young lady, and we'll take your temperature. Evan! Get out here and help Dad with her bags."

Jilly didn't have a fever, but Mom made her go to bed, anyway. After Evan finished his chores and had taken care of his 4-H heifer, he went upstairs. One of the dogs, the old spaniel that was Jilly's favorite, lay inside the door. It whimpered as it crept out of Evan's way.

Jilly lay in the exact center of her bed, the sheets folded down over the patchwork quilt that Grandma made the last winter before she died. She looked up at Evan and said, "I'm not afraid of you."

"Of course not." Evan sat on the side of the bed. The mattress springs creaked under his weight. "You've had all summer to make someone else's life miserable."

"You're not my real brother," she whispered.

Maybe the thing to do was humor her. Evan went into his

own room and rummaged in his toy chest. Among the dog-chewed baseballs, the action figures, mismatched Legos, and his favorite model spaceship that Jilly had broken, he found the old hockey goalie mask he'd used as part of his costume last Halloween. He'd painted green slime around the eye-holes and red nail-polish blood dripping from the mouth. The red had faded to orange, but it still looked great. He put it on and lumbered back to Jilly's room, practicing his Frankenstein walk, arms outstretched, legs stiff.

"I am the monster who has taken Evan's place!" he growled in his deepest voice.

Normally, Jilly would have gone, "Eek!" or thrown a pillow at him or even pretended to be some other monster. She did a truly inspired Lady Dracula imitation. But now she sat there, white-faced.

Evan whipped the mask off. "Come on, I was only kidding."

"I wasn't."

The next morning, Jilly still didn't have a temperature. Mom drove her over to play with her best friend, Doris, whose parents owned the farm five miles down the road. Evan hadn't seen their neighbors all summer. He'd been too busy watching sci-fi movies on television, taking apart the old tractor in the shed, and paging through the ency-clopedia. Dad had spent much of the summer at the Air Force base, although Evan didn't know what he did there.

After she brought Jilly back, Doris's mother marched into the kitchen. Mom set Evan to peeling potatoes while she made the meatloaf.

"You've got to do something about that child before she gets out of hand," said Doris's mother. "Spouting nonsense about not belonging. Next thing, she'll claim she was adopted. I saw a case like this on TV. Kid went from bad to worse in no time. The family had to send her to New York City to a special doctor—can you imagine that?"

Mom ran one hand through her fine—mousey hair, which she'd grown out that summer until it covered her shoulders. Evan and Dad had both let theirs grow out, too.

Doris's mother nattered on about cults and perverts and the way computer games twisted kids' minds.

"She's only eight," Mom said in an exasperated voice, "and she stayed with Cousin Edith the whole time."

"Never let her out of her sight for an instant, did she?"

After Doris's mother left, Mom phoned Cousin Edith in Chicago. "Did anything happen to Jilly when she was with you? She's been acting a little strange since she got home . . . I guess you're right, that it was some bug she caught on the plane coming home. You never can tell what kind of spores people carry around these days."

Evan woke suddenly in the middle of the night, startled out of a nightmare of meteor showers and sudden bright colors.

Moonlight streamed through his open window, almost bright enough to read by. The house creaked as it settled. But something in the familiar shadows of his room sent a chill down his spine. He held his breath, listening. Then he heard a faint noise.

Breathing.

Without daring to move more than his eyes, he

scanned the room. He made out a shape, darker than the rest, standing beside his bed. Watching him as he slept.

"Geez, Jilly . . ."

Then she was gone, padding down the hall on her bare feet.

Jilly wasn't sick, that much was certain. There was definitely something wrong with her, something majorly creepy. After last night, Evan had the chilling thought that maybe this wasn't Jilly at all, but a robot which looked just like her. That started him thinking, remembering the movies he'd seen, of lights coming from the sky and snatching people off airplanes in flight, or aliens replacing people with pod creatures. . . .

What had she been doing last night? Studying him, planning a way to take him over or turn him into an alien, too?

Everything started to made sense.

As a test, Evan brought Jilly the new issue of *Astonishing Space Ranger Stories*. This was something of a sacrifice, since he still hadn't forgiven her for snatching his magazines from the mailbox last winter and reading them before he'd had a chance. He didn't mind sharing them afterward, but he wanted to be the one to rip open the plastic cover and peel apart the glossy, ink-smelling pages.

Jilly's door hung partly open. Evan stood in the doorway, watching her before she saw him. She was sitting up, the tray with its untouched hamburger by her side, cradling something in her hands. He moved closer. It was a harvestman spider, the kind that sometimes came into the house late in the summer. Jilly had pulled off three of its legs.

When she saw him, she brushed the spider off the bed.

"What do you want now?" she said.

He handed her the magazine.

Jilly picked it up, and for a moment nothing happened. She just stared at it, her eyes getting bigger and paler, until they looked like marbles of ice. Then she opened her mouth and screamed—a high, tight sound. In one swift movement, she threw the magazine across the room.

Evan scooped it up and ran for the door. Standing in the hallway, his heart beating like a hammer, he smoothed the rumpled cover. The painting showed a flying saucer landing on a field at night, just like in the old movie. Evan's stomach went cold and cheesy. Then he took his notepad and pencil from his jeans pocket and began to write.

After dinner, when Jilly had retreated back to her bedroom, the family talked about what was going on with her. At first Dad blamed the flight back. Jilly was much too young to travel so far alone, he said.

Mom thought she was still having trouble readjusting to being home.

Evan saw his chance. He showed them everything he'd written in his notepad, about the spider and the magazine cover and the way her hair smelled wrong at the airport. He hadn't taken any notes about last night when Jilly had watched him sleep. That was just too creepy to talk about.

"There's only one explanation," he said. "Jilly's been taken over by aliens from outer space!"

Mom said that was ridiculous and Evan had been reading too many scary stories. "Give her a little more time, she'll be fine."

"No," said Dad. "If something is bothering Jilly, we need to get it out in the open."

Dinner the next night was fried chicken, Jilly's favorite, corn on the cob, and three-bean salad. Jilly ate it all. Evan wrote everything down on his notepad. Afterward, Dad called everyone together in the living room and told Jilly how much they loved her and there wasn't anything that she had to hide from them. Jilly listened, hugging her bony, scab-covered knees. She wore a backless sundress that made her look thinner than ever.

"Talk to us, baby." Dad leaned forward. "Whatever's bothering you, you can tell us. We're your family."

"No." Jilly stared back at him with eyes like twin lakes of tears. "You're not my family."

"It's no good talking," said Evan. "I told you—"

"Don't tease, Evan," Dad said. "She's having a hard enough time already."

"Look, ever since she came back, she's been different," Evan persisted. "No matter how much we love her, we can't change that. Jilly, the real Jilly, would never . . . She'd pick a spider up and put it outside so it wouldn't get hurt. And she hates three-bean salad."

"Evan, that's enough," said Dad in his you-better-pay-attention voice.

"Oh, he's so imaginative," Mom said, smiling like a Kmart dummy. "Boys will say anything these days.

Now let's forget all about this UFO business, before we make Jilly worse."

Evan felt desperate—they had to believe him! There was no telling what the alien Jilly would do now that she knew he suspected her. "I showed her a picture of a flying saucer and she threw it at me. She—"

"Stop it!" Jilly cried.

She slid off the chair and walked over to Evan. Her skinny legs shook and her face turned so red her freckles hardly showed at all. "All you know is a bunch of stuff from movies and magazines. You wouldn't know an alien if one was looking out at you from a mirror!"

"That's ridiculous!" Dad said. He looked dark and dangerous, angry in a way that Evan had never seen.

Jilly flinched and dodged behind Evan. "It isn't me that's been taken over by aliens, it's *you!* All of you!"

Evan felt like someone had played snap-the-whip with his mind. What was going on? He decided to try to handle Jilly himself until Dad could calm down.

"It's okay," he said to Dad. "I can talk sense into her." He drew Jilly away from both parents, out toward the hall. "Let me get this straight," he said. "You think I'm an alien—and Mom and Dad, too. Doesn't that strike you as a bit strange?"

"I saw the same movies you did, but they had it all wrong. Aliens don't look like pods of fluff or green lights or bug-eyed monsters. They can't walk around on Earth any more than we can on the moon. So they wear some kind of spacesuits. I saw one on your neck that night when you were asleep. Hold still and I'll show you."

107

Jilly put her arms around Evan's neck. Her fingers burrowed beneath his hair, the hair he'd grown long over the summer. The hair that was hiding—no, there was nothing there to hide! He was fine, he told himself, fine. . . .

Jilly combed her fingers through Evan's hair so hard her nails scraped his scalp. He started shaking worse than she was.

"Evan, don't let her," came Dad's voice, sounding as if he were calling from the other end of a football field. "We can't lose you. It's just us three, don't you see? We've lost the other scouts and we can't send a signal with only two units."

Make her stop! The words shrieked through Evan's mind, or maybe it was Dad's voice. *Hit her, push her down, smash her! Quick now, before it's too late—*

But this was Jilly, his baby sister. True, she could be a brat, but he remembered the time she'd given him her double-dip chocolate ice cream cone at the county fair when some older boy had dumped his in the dust, and how she'd listened by the hour to his stories about ghosts and baseball, and no matter what, he couldn't hurt her.

"Do something!" Mom sobbed. "Stop her!"

Out of the corner of one eye, Evan saw Mom start toward them, arms outstretched. Her face looked like a plaster mask, frozen in rage or maybe terror, so that he hardly recognized her.

Before Mom could reach them, Jilly yanked hard on something at the back of Evan's neck. Anchor-barbs came free, stinging where they'd attached to his skull.

He felt as if a network of threads were being pulled from his brain and spinal cord, burning like fire.

Mom screamed, "No!" Outside in the yard, the dogs starting howling.

Evan blinked and looked around. Everything seemed so different, the walls, the furniture, the cornfields beyond the windows. No—it was *he* who'd been different all summer, as if he'd been seeing the world through colored glasses.

Now it all came back to him in a rush of memories, the night after Jilly left, how he went outside with Mom and Dad to watch the meteor shower, the lights falling all around them, and how everything smelled funny the next morning and the dogs barked and wouldn't let them come near.

All the while he'd been thinking Jilly was the alien.

"Jilly, listen to me." There was something odd about Dad's voice, like an echo effect. "If aliens were to come to Earth—and I'm not saying they have—then they might not be bad guys. They might be . . . curious, do you see? They'd want to find out more about us . . ."

To spy on us, Evan thought. *To use us to spy for them.* He thought of all the days Dad had spent down at the Air Force Base, watching the military planes and how he'd wasted his summer on old sci-fi movies and paging through the encyclopedia, passing on all that knowledge.

"I don't care!" Jilly stamped one foot. "I want my Daddy back! I want him back now!"

On the table, something stirred. It looked for all the world like a metallic spider. Each leg ended in dark threads that smoked slightly. Jilly had taken it from the back of Evan's head. He reached up with one hand, half expecting to feel his neck slick with blood, but his fingers met only tender, swollen skin—no worse than a bad sunburn.

"What have you done?" Mom shrieked. "It's useless now! The whole mission is ruined! We can't call the ship with only two. We'll be stranded on this desolate planet forever!"

"No, it's not too late," Dad said. "The unit is damaged, but it can be implanted in a new host. The girl is not as good for our purposes as the boy—she's younger and weaker—but we can't use him again. She'll have to do.

"You want to get your family back?" Dad smiled at Jilly, not at all a nice smile. "In just a minute, you will join them."

Dad put his hands on Jilly's shoulders, pushing her toward the table. She whimpered, "No," and tried to twist free, but she wasn't strong enough. He kept talking in that same voice, as if he were trying to hypnotize her.

"It isn't so bad," he repeated. "You'll see."

On the table, the spider-thing—the alien probe or whatever it was—moved, first one long, jointed leg and then another. It had ten of them, the two longest ending in hooks that glistened as if they were wet with slime. It lifted itself and crept toward the edge of the table . . . toward Jilly's bare back.

"You'll see . . ." Dad repeated, like a tape loop. "You'll see . . ."

Jilly choked out the words, "Please, Daddy, don't."

The two longer legs caught in the skirt of her dress,

barely creasing the cloth. It hauled itself up as if it weighed nothing.

All Evan had to do was to reach up and grab the thing. Pull it apart like Jilly had the harvestman spiders or stamp it into the floor.

The aliens hadn't hurt any of them, had they? Maybe Dad was right—they were just curious. But maybe they'd come back to conquer Earth if they found it an easy target. Then he remembered how dark Dad had looked, how he'd shouted at Jilly, scaring her half to death. He remembered the expression on Mom's face.

Evan wished he could think straight. He didn't know who he could trust. Was it Dad talking or the alien speaking through him? What about the magazine stories about green scaly monsters and brains in jars? Were they just some crazy writer's imagination or were they a warning?

"I want my family back," Jilly had said.

My family, too, he thought.

Evan couldn't remember Jilly ever backing off when she said something in that tone of voice. She wouldn't whine or plead—she just wouldn't give up. He remembered the way she fought over eating three-bean salad and how she stopped snatching his magazines from the mailbox when she was good and ready, not before.

The aliens might have all kinds of mind-control devices, fancy meteor spaceships, and cosmic weapons. Evan decided that once Jilly got an idea in her head, the aliens didn't stand a chance.

He got to his feet and closed his fingers around the

spidery shape. The legs crumpled like eggshells in his hand, leaving little stinging scratches. A high, thin whining gradually faded.

"Come on, Dad," Evan said as gently as he dared.

Dad hung his head, his shoulders quivering as if he were sobbing silently. He didn't pull away when Evan reached up to the back of his neck. It was as if whatever drove him had given up.

Evan felt beneath Dad's springy hair and touched skin sticky with sweat. Ridges ran alongside Dad's spine, with a lump near the base of his skull. In the center of the lump, Evan's fingers touched hard, smooth metal. It came free when he dug beneath it, the anchoring legs snapping as they came loose. Getting the thing off Dad was easier than he'd thought. He put it on the table. Mom stood quietly as Jilly removed hers, too.

Already Evan's thoughts were clearing. In a few minutes, Mom and Dad would start to become themselves, too. Maybe in time they'd all forget what had happened to them. Maybe they wouldn't. One thing he knew for certain; the aliens wouldn't be coming back. Their probe had failed and they'd have to find another system, another planet.

Jilly yanked the spider-thing from Mom and turned toward Evan with a grin. He supposed there were worse things than having Earth's secret weapon for a baby sister, and grinned back at her.

WHY I LEFT HARRY'S ALL-NIGHT HAMBURGERS

by Lawrence Watt-Evans

Harry's was a nice place—probably still is. I haven't been back lately. It's a couple of miles off I-79, a few exits north of Charleston, near a place called Sutton. Used to do a pretty fair business until they finished building the Interstate out from Charleston and made it worthwhile for some fast-food joints to move in right next to the cloverleaf; nobody wanted to drive the extra miles to Harry's after that. Folks used to wonder how old Harry stayed in business, as a matter of fact, but he did all right even without the Interstate trade. I found that out when I worked there.

Why did I work there, instead of at one of the fast-food joints? Because my folks lived in a little house just around the corner from Harry's, out in the middle of nowhere—not in Sutton itself, just out there on the road. Wasn't anything around except our house and Harry's place. He lived out back of his restaurant. That was about the only thing I could walk to in under an hour, and I didn't have a car.

This was when I was sixteen. I needed a job, because my dad was out of work again and if I was gonna do anything I needed my own money. Mom didn't mind my using her car—so long as it came back with a full tank of gas and I didn't keep it too long. That was the rule. So I needed some work, and Harry's All-Night

Hamburgers was the only thing within walking distance. Harry said he had all the help he needed—two cooks and two people working the counter, besides himself. The others worked days, two to a shift, and Harry did the late night stretch all by himself. I hung out there a little, since I didn't have anywhere else, and it looked like pretty easy work—there was hardly any business, and those guys mostly sat around telling dirty jokes. So I figured it was perfect.

Harry, though, said that he didn't need any help.

I figured that was probably true, but I wasn't going to let logic keep me out of driving my mother's car. I did some serious begging, and after I'd made his life miserable for a week or two Harry said he'd take a chance and give me a shot, working the graveyard shift, midnight to eight A.M., as his counterman, busboy, and janitor all in one.

I talked him down to 7:30, so I could still get to school, and we had us a deal. I didn't care about school so much myself, but my parents wanted me to go, and it was a good place to see my friends, y'know? Meet girls and so on.

So I started working at Harry's, nights. I showed up at midnight the first night, and Harry gave me an apron and a little hat, like something from a diner in an old movie, same as he wore himself. I was supposed to wait tables and clean up, not cook, so I don't know why he wanted me to wear them, but he gave them to me, and I needed the bucks, so I put them on and pretended I didn't notice that the apron was all stiff with grease and smelled like something nasty had died on it a few weeks back. And Harry—he's a funny old guy, always looked fiftyish, as far back as I can remember. Never young, but never getting really old, either, y'know? Some people do that, they just seem to go on forever. Anyway, he showed me where everything was in the kitchen and back room, told me to keep busy cleaning up whatever looked like it wanted cleaning, and told me, over and over again, like he was really worried that I was going to cause trouble.

"Don't bother the customers. Just take their orders, bring them their food, and don't bother them. You got that?"

"Sure," I said. "I got it."

"Good," he said. "We get some funny guys in here at night, but they're good customers, most of them, so don't you screw up with anyone. One customer complains, one customer stiffs you for the check, and you're out of work, you got that?"

"Sure," I said, though I've gotta admit I was wondering what to do if some cheapskate skipped without paying. I tried to figure how much of a meal would be worth paying for in order to keep the job, but with taxes and all it got too tricky for me to work out, and I decided to wait until the time came, if it ever did.

Then Harry went back in the kitchen, and I got a broom and swept up out front a little until a couple of truckers came in and ordered burgers and coffee.

I was pretty awkward at first, but I got the hang of it after a little bit. Guys would come in, women, too, one or two at a time, and they'd order something, and Harry'd have it ready faster than you can say "cheese," practically. They'd eat it, and wipe their mouths, and drive off, and none of them said a thing to me except their orders, and I didn't say anything back except "Yes, sir," or "Yes, ma'am," or "Thank you, come again." I figured they were all just truckers who didn't like the fast-food places.

That was what it was like at first, anyway, from midnight to about one, one-thirty, but then things would slow down. Even the truckers were off the roads by then, I guess, or they didn't want to get that far off the Interstate, or they'd all had lunch, or something. Anyway, by about two that first night I was thinking it was pretty clear why Harry didn't think he needed help on this shift, when the door opened and the little bell rang.

I jumped a bit—that bell startled me. I started to turn around, but then I looked at Harry, 'cause I'd seen him out of the corner of my eye. He'd gotten this worried look on his face, and *he* was watching *me*. He wasn't looking at the customer at all.

About then I realized that the reason the bell had startled me was that I hadn't heard anyone drive up. And who was going to be out walking to Harry's place at two in the morning in the West Virginia mountains? The way Harry was looking at me, I knew this must be one of those special customers he didn't want me to scare away.

So I turned around, and there was this short little guy in a really heavy coat, all zipped up, made of that shiny silver fabric you see race-car drivers wear, you know? He was just putting down the hood. He was wearing padded ski pants of the same stuff, with pockets all over the place. Over his eyes were big, thick goggles like he'd been out in a blizzard, but it was April and there hadn't been any snow in weeks. It was about fifty or sixty degrees outside.

Well, I didn't want to blow it, so I pretended I didn't notice. I just said, "Hello, sir. May I take your order?"

He looked at me funny and said, "I suppose so."

"Would you like to see a menu?" I said, trying to be on my best behavior. I was probably overdoing it; I'd let the truckers find their own menus.

"I suppose so," he said again, and I handed him the menu.

He looked it over, and pointed to a picture of a cheeseburger that looked about as much like anything from Harry's grill as Sly Stallone looks like me. I wrote down the order and passed the slip back to Harry.

"Don't bother the guy!" Harry hissed at me.

I took the hint, and went back to sweeping until the burger was up. As I was handing the plate to the guy, there was a sound out front like a shotgun going off, and this green light flashed in through the window. I nearly dropped the plate. I couldn't go look outside because the customer was digging through his pockets for money, to pay for the burger.

"You can pay after you've eaten, sir," I said.

"I will pay first," he said, real formal. "I may need to depart quickly. My money may not be good here."

The guy hadn't any accent, but with that remark about the money I figured he was a foreigner, so I waited. He hauled out a handful of weird coins and passed them over to me.

"I'll need to check with the manager," I told him.

"I *told* you I get some strange customers, kid," Harry said when I went back to the kitchen to talk to him. "Let's see the money." So I gave him the coins, and he said, "Yeah, we'll take these," and made change—I don't know how, because the writing on the coins looked like Russian to me, and I couldn't figure out what any of them were.

He gave me the change, and then looked me in the eye. "You think you can handle the counter without losing me any customers, or do you want to call it a night and find another job?"

I really wanted that paycheck. I gritted my teeth and said, "No problem!"

Around four A.M., things slowed down again, and around four-thirty or five, the breakfast crowd began to trickle in, but between two and four there were about half a dozen customers, I guess. I don't remember who they all were any more, most of them weren't that strange, but that first little guy, him I remember. Maybe some of the others were pretty strange, too, maybe stranger than the first guy, but he was the *first*, which makes a difference.

When I got off at seven-thirty, I was all mixed up; I didn't know *what* was going on. I was beginning to think maybe I imagined it all.

I went home and changed clothes, then caught the bus to school. What with not really having adjusted to working nights, and being tired, and having to think about schoolwork, I was pretty much convinced that the whole experience at the diner had been some weird dream. When I came home after classes, I slept through until about eleven, then got up and went to work again.

It was almost the same scene, except that there weren't midgets in ski parkas. The normal truckers and the rest came in first, then they faded out.

And then the weirdos started turning up again around two o'clock.

At sixteen, you know, you think you can cope with anything—at least, *I* did. So I didn't let the customers bother me, not even the ones who didn't look like they were exactly human beings. Harry got used to me being there, and I did make it a lot easier on him. After the first couple of weeks it was pretty much settled that I could stay on for as long as I liked.

I liked it fine, really, once I got used to the weird hours. I didn't have much of a social life during the week—never really had one, living where I did—and I could afford to do the weekends up in style with what Harry paid me and the tips I got. Some of those tips I had to take to the jewelers in Charleston—different ones each time, so nobody would notice that one guy was bringing in all these odd coins and trinkets. Harry gave me some pointers—he'd been doing the same thing for years, except that he'd visited every jeweler in West

Virginia, from Charleston to Huntington to Wheeling. He'd also done business with a bunch in Washington, D.C., and Philadelphia. He was halfway through the Pittsburgh jewelers now.

It was fun, really, seeing just what would turn up at the diner and order a burger. I think my favorite was the guy who walked in—no car, no lights, no nothing—wearing this electric-blue hunter's vest with wires all over it, and these medieval tights with what Harry called a codpiece. There was snow and some kind of sticky goop all over his vest and in his hair. He was shivering like it was the Arctic out there, when it was the middle of July. He had some kind of little animal crawling around under that vest, but he wouldn't let me get a look at it; from the shape of the bulge it made it might have been a weasel or something. He had the strangest accent you ever heard, but he acted right at home and ordered without looking at the menu.

Harry admitted, when I'd been there awhile, that he figured anyone else would mess things up for him somehow. I might have thought I was going nuts, or I might have called the cops, or I might have spread a lot of strange stories around, but I didn't, and Harry appreciated that.

Hey, that was easy. If these people didn't bother Harry, I figured, why should they bother me? And it wasn't anybody else's business, either. When people asked, I used to tell them that, sure, we got weirdos in the place late at night—but I never said just how weird.

121

But I never got as cool about it as Harry was—I mean, a flying saucer in the parking lot wouldn't make Harry blink. *I* blinked, when we got 'em—not very often, though—and I had to really work not to stare at them. Most of the customers had more sense; if they came in something strange they hid it in the woods or something. But there were always a few who couldn't be bothered. If any state cops ever cruised past there and saw those things, I guess they didn't dare report them. No one would've believed them, anyway.

I asked Harry once if all these guys came from the same place.

"Haven't got a clue," he said. He'd never asked, and he didn't want me to, either, in case asking too many questions might chase 'em off.

Except he was wrong about thinking that would scare them away. Sometimes you can tell when someone wants to talk, and some of these people did. So I talked to them.

I think I was seventeen by the time someone told me what was really going on.

Before you ask any stupid questions, no, they weren't any of them Martians or monsters from outer space or anything like that. Some of them were from West Virginia, in fact. Just not *our* West Virginia. Lots of different West Virginias, instead. What the science-fiction writers call "parallel worlds." That's one name, anyway. Other dimensions, alternate realities—they have lots of different names for it.

It all makes sense, really. A couple of the customers explained it to me. See, everything that ever could possibly have happened, in the entire history of the universe right from the Big Bang up until now, *did* happen—somewhere. And *every* possible difference means a different universe. Not just if Napoleon lost at Waterloo, or won, or whatever he didn't do here. (What does Napoleon matter to the *universe*, anyway?)

But every single atom or particle or whatever, whenever it had a chance to do something—break up or stay together, or move one direction instead of another, whatever—it did in all of them, but in different universes. They didn't branch off, either—all the universes were always there, there just wasn't any difference between them until this particular event came along. That means that there are millions and millions of identical universes, too, where the differences haven't happened yet. There's an infinite number of universes—more than that, an infinity of infinities. I mean, you can't really comprehend it; if you think you're close, then multiply that a few zillion times. *Everything* is out there.

In a lot of those universes, people figured out how to travel from one dimension to another; apparently, it's not that hard. There are lots of different ways to do it, too, which is why everything from guys in street clothes to people in spacesuits and flying saucers showed up at Harry's.

But there's one thing about the whole travel idea that got me thinking: With an infinite number of universes, how can you find just *one?* Particularly the first time out?

Fact is, you can't. It's just not possible. So the explorers go out, but they don't come back. Maybe if some *did* come back, they could look at what they did and where it took them and figure out how to measure and aim and all that. But so far as any of the ones I've talked to know, nobody has ever done it. When you go out, that's it, you're out there. You can go on hopping from one world to the next, or you can settle down in one forever, but, like the saying goes, you *really* can't go home again.

You can get close, though. I found out a lot of this in exchange for telling this poor old geezer a lot about the world outside Harry's. He was pretty happy about it when I was talking about what I'd seen on TV, and naming all the presidents I could think of, but then he asked me something about some religion he said he belonged to. When I said I'd never heard of it he almost broke down. I guess he was looking for a world like his own, and ours was, you know, close, but not close enough.

He said something about what he called a "Random Walk Principle": If you go wandering around the dimensions at random, you keep coming back close to where you started, but you'll never have your feet in *exactly* the original place. You'll always be a little bit off to one side or the other.

So there are millions of these people out there drifting from world to world, looking for whatever they're looking for. Sometimes millions of them identical to each other, too, and they run into each other. They know what to look for, see. So they trade information, and some of them tell me they're working on figuring out how to really navigate whatever it is they do, and they've figured out some of it already, so they can steer a little.

I wondered out loud once why so many of them turn up at Harry's, and this woman with blue-gray skin—from some kind of medication, she told me—tried to explain it. West Virginia is one of the best places to travel between worlds, particularly up in the mountains around Sutton, because it's a pretty central location for eastern North America, but there isn't anything there. I mean, there aren't any big cities, or big military bases, or anything, so that if there's an atomic war or something—and apparently there have been a *lot* of atomic wars, or wars with even worse weapons, on different worlds—nobody's very likely to heave any missiles at Sutton, West Virginia. Even in the realities where the Europeans never found America and it's the Chinese or somebody building the cities, there just isn't any reason to build anything near Sutton. And there's something that makes it an easy place to travel between worlds, too, although I didn't follow the explanation—something about the Earth's magnetic field. I didn't catch whether that was part of the explanation, or just a comparison of some kind.

The mountains and forests of West Virginia make it easy to hide, too, which is why it's better than out in the desert or someplace open like that.

Anyway, right around Sutton it's pretty safe and easy to travel between worlds, so lots of people do.

The strange thing, though, is that for some reason that nobody really seemed clear on, Harry's—or something like it—is in just about the same place in millions of these different realities. It's not always exactly Harry's All-Night Hamburgers; one customer kept calling Harry "Sal," for instance. It's *here*, though, and the one thing that doesn't seem to change much is that travelers can eat here without causing trouble. Word gets around that Harry's is a nice, quiet place, with decent burgers, where nobody's going to hassle them about anything. Where they can pay in gold or silver if they haven't got the local money, or in trade goods or whatever they've got that Harry can use. One guy told me that Harry's seems to be in more universes than Washington, D.C. He'd even seen one of my doubles before, last time he stopped in, and he thought he might have actually gotten back to the same place until I swore I'd never seen him before. He had these really funny eyes, so I was sure I'd have remembered him.

We never actually got repeat business from other worlds, y'know, not once, not ever; nobody could ever find the way back to exactly our world. What we got were people who had heard about Harry's from other people, in some other reality. Oh, maybe it wasn't exactly the same Harry's they'd heard about, but they'd heard that it was a good place to eat and swap stories.

That's a weird thought, you know, that every time I served someone a burger a zillion of me were serving burgers to a zillion others—not all of them the same, either.

So they come to Harry's to eat, and they trade information with each other in the booths, or at the counter, or in the parking lot, and they take a break from whatever they're doing.

They came, and they talked to me about all those other universes, and I was seventeen years old, man. It was like those Navy recruiting ads on TV: see the world. Except it was see the *worlds*—*all* of them, not just one.

I listened to everything those guys said. I heard them talk about a world where zeppelins strafed Cincinnati in a Third World War. About places where the dinosaurs never died out, and mammals never evolved any higher than rats. About cities built of colored glass or dug miles underground. About worlds where all the men were dead, or all the women, or both, from biological warfare. Any story you ever heard, anything you ever read, those guys could top it. Worlds where speaking aloud could get you the death penalty—not what you said, just saying *anything* out loud. Worlds with spaceships fighting a war against Arcturus. Beautiful women, strange places—everything you could ever want, out there *somewhere*, but it might take forever to find it.

I listened to those stories for months. I graduated from high school, but there wasn't any way I could go to college, since my family could never afford it. So I just stayed on with Harry—it paid enough to live on, anyway. I talked to those people from other worlds, even got inside some of their ships, or time machines, or whatever you want to call them, and I thought about how great it would be to just go roaming from world to world. Any time you don't like the way things are going, just *pop!* and the whole world is different! I could be a white god to the Indians in a world where the Europeans and Asians never reached America, I figured, or find a world where machines do all the work and people just relax and party.

When my eighteenth birthday came and went without any sign I'd ever get out of West Virginia, I began to really think about it, you know? I started asking customers about it. A lot of them told me not to be stupid; a lot just wouldn't talk about it. Some, though . . . some of them thought it was a great idea.

There was one guy, this one night—well, first, it was September, but it was still hot as an August afternoon, even in the middle of the night. Most of my friends were gone—they'd gone off to college, or gotten jobs somewhere, or gotten married, or maybe two out of the three. The other kids were back in school. I'd started sleeping days, from eight in the morning until about four P.M., instead of evenings. Harry's air conditioner was busted, and I really wanted to just leave it all behind and go find myself a better world. So when I heard these two guys talking at one table about whether one of them had extra room in his machine, I sort of listened, when I could, when I wasn't fetching burgers and Cokes.

Now, one of these two I'd seen before—he'd been coming in every so often ever since I started working at Harry's. He looked like an ordinary guy, but he came in about three in the morning and talked to the weirdos like they were all old buddies. I figured he had to be from some other world originally himself, even if he stayed put in ours now. He'd come in about every night for a week or two, then disappear for months, then start turning up again, and I had sort of wondered whether he might have licked the navigation problem all those other people had talked about.

But then I figured, probably not, either he'd stopped jumping from one world to the next, or else it was just a bunch of parallel people coming in, and it probably wasn't ever the same guy at all, really. Usually, when that happened, we'd get two or three at a time, looking like identical twins or something, but there was only just one of this guy, every time, so I figured, like I said, either he hadn't been changing worlds at all, or he'd figured out how to navigate better than anyone else, or something.

The guy he was talking to was new; I'd never seen him before. He was big, maybe six-four and heavy. He'd come in shaking snow and soot off a plastic coverall of some kind, given me a big grin, and ordered two of Harry's biggest burgers, with everything. Five minutes later the regular customer sat down across the table from him, and now he was telling the regular that he had plenty of room in his ship for anything anyone might want him to haul crosstime.

I figured this was my chance, so when I brought the burgers. I said something real polite, like, "Excuse me, sir, but I couldn't help overhearing. Do you think you'd have room for a passenger?"

The big guy laughed and said, "Sure, kid! I was just

telling Joe here that I could haul him and all his freight. And there'd be room for you, too, if you can make it worth my trouble!"

I said, "I've got money; I've been saving up. What'll it take?"

The big guy gave me a big grin again, but before he could say anything, Joe interrupted.

"Sid," he said, "could you excuse me for a minute? I want to talk to this young fellow for a minute, before he makes a big mistake."

The big guy, Sid, said, "Sure, sure, I don't mind."

So Joe got up, and he yelled to Harry, "Okay if I borrow your counterman for a few minutes?"

Harry yelled back that it was okay. I didn't know what was going on, but I went along, and the two of us went out to this guy's car to talk.

And it really was a car, too—an old Ford van. It was customized, with velvet and bubble windows and stuff, and there was a lot of stuff piled in the back, camping gear and clothes and things, but no sign of machinery or anything. I still wasn't sure, you know, because some of these guys did a really good job of disguising their ships, or time machines, or whatever, but it sure *looked* like an ordinary van, and that's what Joe said it was. He got into the driver's seat, and I got into the passenger seat, and we swiveled around to face each other.

"So," he said. "do you know who all these people are? I mean people like Sid?"

"Sure," I said. "They're from other dimensions, parallel worlds and like that."

He leaned back and looked at me hard, and said, "You know that, huh? Did you know that none of them can ever get home?"

"Yes, I knew that," I told him, acting pretty cocky.

"And you still want to go with Sid to other universes? Even when you know you'll never come home to this universe again?"

"That's right, Mister," I told him. "I'm sick of this one. I don't have anything here but a nothing job in a diner. I want to see some of the stuff these people talk about, instead of just hearing about it."

"You want to see wonders and marvels, huh?"

"Yes!"

"You want to see buildings a hundred stories high? Cities of strange temples? Oceans thousands of miles wide? Mountains miles high? Prairies, and cities, and strange animals and stranger people?"

Well, that was just exactly what I wanted, better than I could have said it myself. "Yes," I said. "You got it, Mister."

"You lived here all your life?"

"You mean this world? Of course I have."

"No, I meant here in Sutton. You lived here all your life?"

"Well, yeah," I admitted. "Just about."

He sat forward and put his hands together, and his voice got intense, like he wanted to impress me with how serious he was. "Kid," he said, "I don't blame you a bit for wanting something different. I sure wouldn't want to spend my entire life in these hills. But you're going about it the wrong way. You don't want to hitch with Sid."

"Oh, yeah?" I said, "Why not? Am I supposed to build my own machine? I can't even fix my mother's carburetor."

"No, that's not what I meant. Kid, you can see those buildings a thousand feet high in New York, or in Chicago. You've got oceans here in your own world as good as anything you'll find anywhere. You've got the mountains, and the seas, and the prairies, and all the rest of it. I've been in your world for eight years now, checking back here at Harry's every so often to see if anyone's figured out how to steer in no-space and get me home, and this dimension is a big, interesting place."

"But," I said, "what about the spaceships, and—"

He interrupted me, and said, "You want to see spaceships? You go to Florida and watch a shuttle launch. Man, that's a spaceship. It may not go to other worlds, but that *is* a spaceship. You want strange animals? You go to Australia or Brazil. You want strange people? Go to New York or Los Angeles, or almost anywhere. You want a city carved out of a mountaintop? It's called Machu Picchu, in Peru, I think. You want ancient, mysterious ruins? They're all over Greece and Italy and North Africa. Strange temples? Visit India; there are supposed to be over a thousand temples in Benares alone. See Angkor Wat, or the pyramids—not just the Egyptian ones, but the Mayan ones, too.

"And the great thing about all of these places, kid," he continued, "is that afterwards, if you want to, you can come home. You don't *have* to, but you *can*. Who knows? You might get homesick someday. Most people do. *I* did. I wish I'd seen more of my own world before I volunteered to try any others."

I kind of stared at him for a while. "I don't know," I said. I mean, it seemed so easy to just hop in Sid's machine and be gone forever, I thought, but New York was five hundred miles away—and then I realized how stupid that was.

"Hey," he said, "don't forget: if you decide I was wrong, you can always come back to Harry's and bum a ride with someone. It won't be Sid, he'll be gone forever, but you'll find someone. Most world-hoppers are lonely, kid; they've left behind everyone they ever knew. You won't have any trouble getting a lift."

Well, that decided it, because, y'know, he was obviously right about that, as soon as I thought about it. I told him so.

"Well, good!" he said, "Now, you go pack your stuff and apologize to Harry and all that, and I'll give you a lift to Pittsburgh. You've got money to travel with from there, right? These idiots still haven't figured out how to steer, so I'm going back home—not my *real* home, but where I live in your world—and I wouldn't mind a passenger."

And he smiled at me. And I smiled back.

We had to wait until the bank opened the next morning, but he didn't really mind. All the way to Pittsburgh, he was singing these hymns and war songs from his home world, where there was a second civil war in the 1920's because of some fundamentalist preacher trying to overthrow the Constitution and set up a church government. Joe hadn't had anyone he could sing them to in years, he said.

That was six years ago, and I haven't gone back to Harry's since.

So, that was what got me started traveling. What brings *you* to Benares?

DEBORAH'S CHOICE

by Alethea Eason

I always thought my family was strange, but Willy's family seemed weirder than mine. Willy and I were both in Mr. Bartlett's fifth grade class. I went to his house one day after school to work on a skit about Deborah Sampson, a woman soldier in the Revolutionary War. I chose her because Deborah's the name I go by. It's the closest name in English to my real one, which is impossible for people to pronounce.

Willy was going to be a redcoat. We had to make sure we included at least three facts about the war. I imagined I'd say something like, "Take this for all those brave lads who gave up their lives at Valley Forge," as I bayoneted him in the gut. One fact down.

It was the beginning of October, the first day of Halloween, according to Willy. He was excited because his dad and Margie, his dad's girlfriend, just announced they were getting married. I was the only kid at school who knew that the wedding was going to take place at ten minutes before midnight on Halloween in the Prattville graveyard.

Of course I thought this was a bit odd, but I wasn't prepared for what I saw as I walked into their living room. Willy's family didn't have a couch. Instead, a set of three coffins were lined up in front of their television set. Each had a big pillow for a backrest. I could tell which coffin was Willy's right away; it was the shortest. I wondered if he grew out of his coffin the way I did shoes, and had to have a new one every six months or so.

Willy saw the look on my face. "They're really comfortable. It's a shame to waste them on the dead." He said this like it was the family's standard response to all their guests.

Since it was a nice day, we went out to the patio to work. Margie brought us glasses of lemonade. I put mine to the side, hoping I didn't appear rude. I had expected her to look like an Elvira wannabe. I was disappointed when she turned out to be the standard mom, a little chubby, with a bright, cheerful smile. The only thing that gave away her fondness for the season was a pair of skeleton earrings that hung down to her shoulders. But heck, our school secretary had some just like them.

She listened to the ideas we had so far. I mean, she really *listened.* She crossed her arms and a little wrinkle appeared on her forehead to show she was thinking.

"You need more dramatic tension."

"Like what?" I asked.

"Well, except for Native Americans, we're all immigrants in this country."

I felt myself grow red. My family were immigrants. I guess you could say we were *illegal* immigrants. Though we had "assimilated" (a word on next Friday's spelling test), the government didn't know we were here, though no one would ever have guessed. My parents spoke English flawlessly, along with several other languages, including Chinese. I never found out how they learned that one, but Mom said it would come in handy when the others arrived.

There were just a couple of things that would give away our origin, which we spent a considerable amount of effort hiding.

"During the Revolution, only about a third of the population supported it," Margie said. "A third didn't have strong feelings one way or the other, and a third supported the British."

"So?" Willy asked.

"Well, if the young man that Deborah kills was a childhood friend, you've created a richer story."

"The skit is only supposed to last a minute," Willy said. "It's not an epic."

"No, but we've got our second fact," I said. "Thanks, Margie."

Willy found our third fact in an encyclopedia: the British soldiers forced themselves into the homes of the colonists, making them house and feed them. Then, they'd rip off stuff like their milk cows and chickens.

"Made people angry," Willy said, "especially when they took the food."

By the time I left, we had a script.

When I came home, my parents were shut up in the den. The door was closed and their voices were muffled, but my dad sounded excited.

"It's time!" I heard him shout.

Mom seemed to be arguing with him, but I couldn't make out any more of the conversation. When it sounded like they were finishing, I rushed to the kitchen table and opened my books, pretending I was studying, just in time for them to walk in.

Dad's face was red, the way it gets when he's latched on to an idea he won't let go of. Mom looked as though she had been crying.

"Anything wrong?" I asked.

"No," Dad said.

"Yes," Mom said.

"We'll explain later," Dad said. "I'm glad to see you've finally discovered the importance of homework."

"Uh, Dad . . ."

I tried to get his attention, but he began lecturing for the hundredth time about why I had to learn all about American culture and how I would use this knowledge someday to be a leader among our kind.

"Dad." I pointed to his head.

One of his tentacles had popped out. They do that sometimes when he gets agitated. He reached up and shoved it back in. Mom doesn't let him out of the house without a hat.

Willy and I were due to perform our skit on the fifteenth of Halloween. Willy had begun dating his papers this way. Mr. Bartlett told him to stop. Willy refused, saying it was his constitutional right to celebrate holidays in the way he believed.

"We don't get to the Constitution until March," Mr. Bartlett said.

What really upset him was that since October had started, every few days Willy added something ghoulish to his wardrobe. By the fifteenth, he came to school in a Dracula cape, one of Margie's skeletons dangled from an earlobe, and his hair was frizzed as though he had stuck a finger in a light socket. Margie had painted his fingernails black. They were especially long because he hadn't cut them since July.

Willy had promised me that he'd take everything off except the nail polish when it came time to do the skit. Margie had even found a red jacket at a garage sale for him to wear. The question was would Willy still be in class.

"Remove those items now," Mr. Bartlett ordered, "and comb your hair."

"I have the right to wear what I want. It's guaranteed in the Bill of Rights."

"My classroom is not a democracy. Take those things off, or you'll go to the principal's office."

Willy stood up with more dignity than I thought possible, considering how he was dressed, flung his backpack over his shoulder, and walked out of the room.

The class was silent. *There goes my A,* I thought.

Willy didn't return. I ended up doing the skit with Gregory Green, who was an okay alternate, but he didn't have Willy's flair for acting. Willy and I had everything memorized, but Gregory, of course, needed to read from the script.

Deborah's Choice

DEBORAH: Curse you, Johnny, for betraying your people. You've joined the British army and have stolen all our winter provisions. How dare you wear that red coat!

JOHNNY: I believe in the King's cause. As do my parents. Not everyone in the colonies are rebels like you. This food is needed *(Johnny pulls out a chicken from a bag)* for the troops loyal to Britain.

Though Gregory's reading was lackluster, he pulled out the rubber chicken on cue.

DEBORAH: The battle rages over the hill. *(Deborah puts her hand to her ear).*

JOHNNY: I must join the King's forces.

DEBORAH: Oh, no you don't. Even though I grew up with you *(dramatic tension)*, I can't allow you to steal from us. Take this for all the brave lads who gave up their lives at Valley Forge. *(Deborah stabs Johnny. Johnny dies.)*

I had to use several paper towel rolls taped end to end to fake the bayonet, but I think it was effective enough. Gregory fell to the floor, and the class cheered.

I got my A after all, but it belonged to Willy as much as it did to me.

After school I went to Willy's house. Margie let me in. Willy's dad was sitting in one of the coffins talking to someone on the telephone. The living room was now draped with spiders webs and plastic bats hung from the ceiling like Christmas ornaments.

"He's phoning the American Civil Liberties Union to see if we can get a lawyer to argue our case," Margie said. She was beginning to look more like Morticia than Elvira. Her long black dress rustled as she led me to the kitchen. "We're going to fight Willy's suspension."

Willy was at the counter. I sat next to him. Margie put a plate of chocolate chip cookies between us and went back into the living room.

"Sorry about what happened," I said.

"Did you do the skit?"

"Gregory took your part, but I wished you had been there. The kids loved the chicken." I was trying to cheer him up.

"We should have chopped its head off and had fake blood dribble out of the neck."

"That would have been cool."

Willy picked up a cookie. "You're not eating any of these?"

I had to think of something fast. "I don't want to spoil my appetite."

"You're kidding."

I just smiled and shook my head.

"Do you think your parents would let you come to the wedding?" Willy looked so earnest.

"I'm invited?"

"Your whole family can come, if they want," Margie called from her coffin.

My parents had such old-world views I wasn't sure I could talk them into it, but I decided I was going to try. The night in question was a little dicey, but I figured they might be able to fit it into their plans.

To my surprise, Dad said he'd be delighted to go, but then a tentacle popped out. I should have figured out what was going on.

The big day was on a Saturday. Willy called me twice. The first time he was excited about the wedding details. The cake had just arrived. The frosting was all black and there was a vampire bride and groom on top.

Willy was going trick-or-treating before they went to the cemetery. He asked if I wanted to go along.

"I'm sorry. Family plans," I said.

The second time he was even more excited. A lawyer for the ACLU had just called to say he'd take his case. Willy would be going back to school dressed like the other kids on Monday, but he had seven more years in the Prattville school system to deal with.

That afternoon, Mom called me into her bedroom. Since it was Halloween, I wasn't surprised that she let a few tentacles protrude. My family doesn't have a thing for Halloween, but it's convenient for us. Our metabolism is slow, so we need to feed only once a year. Since people think we're in costume, we use the night to our advantage.

Mom and Dad have always gone out and brought back food for me, but Mom told me that Dad had decided that I was old enough to hunt for myself. She said she wanted to protect me a little longer, but she had to accept that I was growing up.

"I know how fond you are of the humans," Mom said. "It's getting harder for me each year. They can be so endearing. But your dad reminded me that the rest of us will be here soon."

"He says that every year."

"I know, dear," she said, reaching out to stroke me, "but you know he's right. When the rest get here, we'll have to conquer the planet. There won't be any room to be sentimental."

I thought about what I had been learning in history. "But, Mom, that's no way for a democracy to work."

"The home world is not a democracy."

Mr. Bartlett came to mind. Maybe we could eat him. Then I knew what Dad was planning.

"Mom, I can't eat Willy's family."

Mom crossed two of her tentacles. "Sweetie, you're going to have to do a lot of things you don't like before long."

I tried not to think of our feeding frenzy, about what I had to do to survive. But every year when Mom and Dad brought dinner home, my DNA took over and I ate until the sun came up. After a few days, it always seemed like it never happened. Up until now, it wasn't personal. I never ate anyone I knew. They were always very careful about that.

Later that night, my parents dragged me to the cemetery. The theme seemed to be vampires. I felt out of place with my tentacles sticking out.

Willy's job was to welcome the guests. He was also going to be his dad's best man. He looked nice in his tuxedo with his hair slicked back. The white makeup and fangs became him. My stomachs started to rumble. As much as I didn't want to, I was getting hungry. I told myself I wouldn't feed, no matter what happened, but deep down I knew once it had begun I wouldn't be able to stop myself.

You can't get better dramatic tension than this, I thought. *Classmate eats best friend for the good of her species.*

Willy came up to us. "Great costumes. Look, we're about to start. I'll talk to you later."

"Sure thing," I said.

A funeral march began to drift eerily over the gravestones. I nudged my way up in front so that I could see. Willy and his dad stood underneath a black awning that had "Margie and Fred, Forever" written on it in fluorescent paint that sparkled in the moonlight.

Margie glided out of a crypt to our left. Everyone let out a sigh. She looked beautiful. She wore a black lace wedding gown and a veil made out of diaphanous webbing. She carried a bouquet of black lilies.

The two of them had written their own vows, all about loving and cherishing and promising to haunt the other when death did them part. I was getting more and more nervous because I knew as soon as they kissed, my parents were going to pounce.

Out of the corner of my eye, I saw one of Dad's tentacles hover over the old guy next to me. Margie's father, I found out later. I could see the rows of teeth being exposed. It was all I could do to keep my tentacles shut.

Just then, a floodlight hit us. Dad withdrew the tentacle fast. A voice called out from a bullhorn: *"Just what do you think you're doing there?"*

In all the confusion of the wedding plans, they forgot to get a permit to use the cemetery. Police were everywhere, but it didn't take long to get things worked out. Pretty soon the officers were chowing down on wedding cake. My parents and I were starving, but now that the authorities were there we had to lie low.

I couldn't help what happened next. Mom said it's because I'm growing and when I have to eat, I have to eat. I followed one of the policemen to his car. My tentacles encircled him, and I began to feed.

My parents were able to get me out of there before anyone saw me. We fed on what was left on the way home, and got back just before another policeman knocked on our door. He told us one of the officers was missing, and he wanted to check to see if we were okay.

Mom had just enough time to throw a hat on Dad's head. It bobbled a bit, but the policeman didn't notice. "We decided not to stay for the reception. It's way past our daughter's bedtime."

Actually, I was ready for bed by then. There was just one problem.

"I'm still hungry," I said on the way to my room.

Mom kissed me good night. "I'm sure something will work out, dear."

Willy was at school on Monday. He ran up to me on the playground.

"Thanks for coming to the wedding," he said. "I looked for you after the ceremony."

"My parents wanted to get me home."

"Weird about that policeman, huh? They still haven't found him."

My stomachs growled at the thought. One human for the three of us just hadn't been enough. "Yeah, weird."

The bell rang, and we walked to class together.

"Hey, Margie wants to know if you and your folks would like to come over for Thanksgiving dinner," Willy said as we lined up.

It was then I made my decision. Mom was right. I couldn't afford to be sentimental. Thanksgiving was what—three weeks away? I could hold out that long.

"We'd be glad to," I said. "Tell her we'll bring dessert."

DARK THEY WERE, AND GOLDEN-EYED

by Ray Bradbury

The rocket metal cooled in the meadow winds. Its lid gave a bulging *pop*. From its clock interior stepped a man, a woman, and three children. The other passengers whispered away across the Martian meadow, leaving the man alone among his family.

The man felt his hair flutter and the tissues of his body draw tight as if he were standing at the center of a vacuum. His wife, before him, seemed almost to whirl away in smoke. The children, small seeds, might at any instant be sown to all the Martian climes.

The children looked up at him, as people look to the sun to tell what time of their life it is. His face was cold.

"What's wrong?" asked his wife.

"Let's get back on the rocket."

"Go back to Earth?"

"Yes! Listen!"

The wind blew as if to flake away their identities. At any moment the Martian air might draw his soul from him, as marrow comes from a white bone. He felt submerged in a chemical that could dissolve his intellect and burn away his past.

They looked at Martian hills that time had worn with a crushing pressure of years. They saw the old cities, lost in their meadows, lying like children's delicate bones among the blowing lakes of grass.

"Chin up, Harry," said his wife. "It's too late. We've come over sixty million miles."

The children with their yellow hair hollered at the deep dome of Martian sky. There was no answer but the racing hiss of wind through the stiff grass.

He picked up the luggage in his cold hands. "Here we go," he said—a man standing on the edge of a sea, ready to wade in and be drowned.

They walked into town.

Their name was Bittering. Harry and his wife Cora; Dan, Laura, and David. They built a small white cottage and ate good breakfasts there, but the fear was never gone. It lay with Mr. Bittering and Mrs. Bittering, a third unbidden partner at every midnight talk, at every dawn awakening.

"I feel like a salt crystal," he said, "in a mountain stream, being washed away. We don't belong here. We're Earth people. This is Mars. It was meant for Martians. For heaven's sake, Cora, let's buy tickets for home!"

But she only shook her head. "One day the atom bomb will fix Earth. Then we'll be safe here."

"Safe and insane!"

Tick-tock, seven o'clock sang the voice-clock; *time to get up*. And they did.

Something made him check everything each morning—warm hearth, potted blood-geraniums—precisely as if he expected something to be amiss. The morning paper was toast-warm from the 6 A.M. Earth rocket. He broke its seal and tilted it at his breakfast place. He forced himself to be convivial.

"Colonial days all over again," he declared. "Why, in ten years there'll be a million Earthmen on Mars. Big cities, everything! They said we'd fail. Said the Martians would resent our invasion. But did we find any Martians? Not a living soul! Oh, we found their empty cities, but no one in them. Right?"

A river of wind submerged the house. When the windows ceased rattling Mr. Bittering swallowed and looked at the children.

"I don't know," said David. "Maybe there're Martians around we don't see. Sometimes nights I think I hear 'em. I hear the wind. The sand hits my window. I get scared. And I see those towns way up in the mountains where the Martians lived a long time ago. And I think I see things moving around those towns, Papa. And I wonder if those Martians *mind* us living here. I wonder if they won't do something to us for coming here."

"Nonsense!" Mr. Bittering looked out the windows. "We're clean, decent people." He looked at his children. "All dead cities have some kind of ghosts in them. Memories, I mean." He stared at the hills. "You see a staircase and you wonder what the Martians looked like climbing it. You see Martian paintings and you wonder what the painter was like. You make a little ghost in your mind, a memory. It's quite natural. Imagination." He stopped. "You haven't been prowling up in those ruins, have you?"

"No, Papa." David looked at his shoes.

"See that you stay away from them. Pass the jam."

152

"Just the same," said little David, "I bet something happens."

Something happened that afternoon.

Laura stumbled through the settlement, crying. She dashed blindly onto the porch.

"Mother, Father—the war, Earth!" she sobbed. "A radio flash just came. Atom bombs hit New York! All the space rockets blown up. No more rockets to Mars, ever!"

"Oh, Harry!" The mother held onto her husband and daughter.

"Are you sure, Laura?" asked the father quietly.

Laura wept. "We're stranded on Mars, forever and ever!"

For a long time there was only the sound of the wind in the late afternoon.

Alone, thought Bittering. Only a thousand of us here. No way back. No way. No way. Sweat poured from his face and his hands and his body; he was drenched in the hotness of his fear. He wanted to strike Laura, cry, "No, you're lying! The rockets will come back!" Instead, he stroked Laura's head against him and said, "The rockets will get through someday."

"Father, what will we do?"

"Go about our business, of course. Raise crops and children. Wait. Keep things going until the war ends and the rockets come again."

The two boys stepped out onto the porch.

"Children," he said, sitting there, looking beyond them, "I've something to tell you."

"We know," they said.

In the following days, Bittering wandered often through the garden to stand alone in his fear. As long as the rockets had spun a silver web across space, he had been able to accept Mars. For he had always told himself: Tomorrow, if I want, I can buy a ticket and go back to Earth.

But now: The web gone, the rockets lying in jigsaw heaps of molten girder and unsnaked wire. Earth people left to the strangeness of Mars, the cinnamon dusts and wine airs, to be baked like gingerbread shapes in Martian summers, put into harvested storage by Martian winters. What would happen to him, the others? This was the moment Mars had waited for. Now it would eat them.

He got down on his knees in the flower bed, a spade in his nervous hands. Work, he thought, work and forget.

He glanced up from the garden to the Martian mountains. He thought of the proud old Martian names that had once been on those peaks. Earthmen, dropping from the sky, had gazed upon hills, rivers, Martian seas left nameless in spite of names. Once Martians had built cities, named cities; climbed mountains, named mountains; sailed seas, named seas. Mountains melted, seas drained, cities tumbled. In spite of this, the Earthmen had felt a silent guilt at putting new names to these ancient hills and valleys.

Nevertheless, man lives by symbol and label. The names were given.

Mr. Bittering felt very alone in his garden under the Martian sun, anachronism bent here, planting Earth flowers in a wild soil.

Think. Keep thinking. Different things. Keep your mind free of Earth, the atom war, the lost rockets.

He perspired. He glanced about. No one watching. He removed his tie. Pretty bold, he thought. First your coat off, now your tie. He hung it neatly on a peach tree he had imported as a sapling from Massachusetts.

He returned to his philosophy of names and mountains. The Earthmen had changed names. Now there were Hormel Valleys, Roosevelt Seas, Ford Hills, Vanderbilt Plateaus, Rockefeller Rivers, on Mars. It wasn't right. The American settlers had shown wisdom, using old Indian prairie names: Wisconsin, Minnesota, Idaho, Ohio, Utah, Milwaukee, Waukegan, Osseo. The old names, the old meanings.

Staring at the mountains wildly, he thought: Are you up there? All the dead ones, you Martians? Well, here we are, alone, cut off! Come down, move us out! We're helpless!

The wind blew a shower of peach blossoms.

He put out his sun-browned hand, gave a small cry. He touched the blossoms, picked them up. He turned them, he touched them again and again. Then he shouted for his wife.

"Cora!"

She appeared at a window. He ran to her.

"Cora, these blossoms!"

She handled them.

"Do you see? They're different. They've changed! They're not peach blossoms any more!"

"Look all right to me," she said.

"They're not. They're *wrong!* I can't tell how. An extra petal, a leaf, something, the color, the smell!"

The children ran out in time to see their father hurrying about the garden, pulling up radishes, onions, and carrots from their beds.

"Cora, come look!"

They handled the onions, the radishes, the carrots among them.

"Do they look like carrots?"

"Yes . . . no." She hesitated. "I don't know."

"They're changed."

"Perhaps."

"You know they have! Onions but not onions, carrots but not carrots. Taste: the same but different. Smell: not like it used to be." He felt his heart pounding, and he was afraid. He dug his fingers into the earth. "Cora, what's happening? What is it? We've got to get away from this." He ran across the garden. Each tree felt his touch. "The roses. The roses. They're turning green!"

And they stood looking at the green roses.

And two days later Dan came running. "Come see the cow. I was milking her and I saw it. Come on!"

They stood in the shed and looked at their one cow.

It was growing a third horn.

And the lawn in front of their house very quietly and slowly was coloring itself like spring violets. Seed from Earth but growing up a soft purple.

"We must get away," said Bittering. "We'll eat this stuff and then we'll change—who knows to what? I can't let it happen. There's only one thing to do. Burn this food!"

"It's not poisoned."

"But it is. Subtly, very subtly. A little bit. A very little bit. We mustn't touch it."

He looked with dismay at their house. "Even the house. The wind's done something to it. The air's burned it. The fog at night. The boards, all warped out of shape. It's not an Earthman's house any more."

"Oh, your imagination!"

He put on his coat and tie. "I'm going into town. We've got to do something now. I'll be back."

"Wait, Harry!" his wife cried.

But he was gone.

In town, on the shadowy step of the grocery store, the men sat with their hands on their knees, conversing with great leisure and ease.

Mr. Bittering wanted to fire a pistol in the air.

What are you doing, you fools! he thought. Sitting here! You've heard the news—we're stranded on this planet. Well, move! Aren't you frightened? Aren't you afraid? What are you going to do?

"Hello, Harry," said everyone.

"Look," he said to them. "You did hear the news, the other day, didn't you?"

They nodded and laughed. "Sure. Sure, Harry."

"What are you going to do about it?"

"Do, Harry, do? What *can* we do?"

"Build a rocket, that's what!"

"A rocket, Harry? To go back to all that trouble? Oh, Harry!"

"But you *must* want to go back. Have you noticed the peach blossoms, the onions, the grass?"

"Why, yes, Harry, seems we did," said one of the men.

"Doesn't it scare you?"

"Can't recall that it did much, Harry."

"Idiots!"

"Now, Harry."

Bittering wanted to cry. "You've got to work with me. If we stay here, we'll all change. The air. Don't you smell it? Something in the air. A Martian virus, maybe; some seed, or a pollen. Listen to me!"

They stared at him.

"Sam," he said to one of them.

"Yes, Harry?"

"Will you help me build a rocket?"

"Harry, I got a whole load of metal and some blueprints. You want to work in my metal shop on a rocket, you're welcome. I'll sell you that metal for five hundred dollars. You should be able to construct a pretty tight rocket, if you work alone, in about thirty years."

Everyone laughed.

"Don't laugh."

Sam looked at him with quiet good humor.

"Sam," Bittering said. "Your eyes—"

"What about them, Harry?"

"Didn't they used to be grey?"

"Well now, I don't remember."

"They were, weren't they?"

"Why do you ask, Harry?"

"Because now they're kind of yellow-colored."

"Is that so, Harry?" Sam said, casually.

"And you're taller and thinner—"

"You might be right, Harry."

"Sam, you shouldn't have yellow eyes."

"Harry, what color eyes have *you* got?" Sam said.

"My eyes? They're blue, of course."

"Here you are, Harry." Sam handed him a pocket mirror. "Take a look at yourself."

Mr. Bittering hesitated, and then raised the mirror to his face.

There were little, very dim flecks of new gold captured in the blue of his eyes.

"Now look at what you've done," said Sam a moment later. "You've broken my mirror."

Harry Bittering moved into the metal shop and began to build the rocket. Men stood in the open door and talked and joked without raising their voices. Once in a while they gave him a hand on lifting something. But mostly they just idled and watched him with their yellowing eyes.

"It's suppertime, Harry," they said.

His wife appeared with his supper in a wicker basket.

"I won't touch it," he said. "I'll only eat food from our Deepfreeze. Food that came from Earth. Nothing

159

from our garden."

His wife stood watching him. "You can't build a rocket."

"I worked in a shop once, when I was twenty. I know metal. Once I get it started, the others will help," he said, not looking at her, laying out the blueprints.

"Harry, Harry," she said, helplessly.

"We've got to get away, Cora. We've *got* to!"

The nights were full of wind that blew down the empty moonlit sea meadows past the little white chess cities lying for their twelve-thousandth year in the shallows. In the Earthmen's settlement, the Bittering house shook with a feeling of change.

Lying abed, Mr. Bittering felt his bones shifted, shaped, melted like gold. His wife, lying beside him, was dark from many sunny afternoons. Dark she was, and golden-eyed, burnt almost black by the sun, sleeping, and the children metallic in their beds, and the wind roaring forlorn and changing through the old peach trees, the violet grass, shaking out green rose petals.

The fear would not be stopped. It had his throat and heart. It dripped in a wetness of the arm and the temple and the trembling palm.

A green star rose in the east.

A strange word emerged from Mr. Bittering's lips.

"Iorrt. Iorrt." He repeated it.

It was a Martian word. He knew no Martian.

In the middle of the night he arose and dialed a call through to Simpson, the archeologist.

"Simpson, what does the word *Iorrt* mean?"

"Why that's the old Martian word for our planet Earth. Why?"

"No special reason."

The telephone slipped from his hand.

"Hello, hello, hello, hello," it kept saying while he sat gazing out at the green star. "Bittering? Harry, are you there?"

The days were full of metal sound. He laid the frame of the rocket with the reluctant help of three indifferent men. He grew very tired in an hour or so and had to sit down.

"The altitude," laughed a man.

"Are you *eating*, Harry?" asked another.

"I'm eating," he said, angrily.

"From your Deepfreeze?"

"Yes!"

"You're getting thinner, Harry."

"I'm not!"

"And taller."

"Liar!"

His wife took him aside a few days later. "Harry, I've used up all the food in the Deepfreeze. There's nothing left. I'll have to make sandwiches using food grown on Mars."

He sat down heavily.

"You must eat," she said. "You're weak."

"Yes," he said.

He took a sandwich, opened it, looked at it, and

began to nibble at it.

"And take the rest of the day off," she said. "It's hot. The children want to swim in the canals and hike. Please come along."

"I can't waste time. This is a crisis!"

"Just for an hour," she urged. "A swim'll do you good."

He rose, sweating. "All right, all right. Leave me alone. I'll come."

"Good for you, Harry."

The sun was hot, the day quiet. There was only an immense staring burn upon the land. They moved along the canal, the father, the mother, the racing children in their swim suits. They stopped and ate meat sandwiches. He saw their skin baking brown. And he saw the yellow eyes of his wife and children, their eyes that were never yellow before. A few tremblings shook him, but were carried off in waves of pleasant heat as he lay in the sun. He was too tired to be afraid.

"Cora, how long have your eyes been yellow?"

She was bewildered. "Always, I guess."

"They didn't change from brown in the last three months?"

She bit her lips. "No. Why do you ask?"

"Never mind."

They sat there.

"The children's eyes," he said. "They're yellow, too."

"Sometimes growing children's eyes change color."

"Maybe *we're* children, too. At least to Mars. That's a thought." He laughed. "Think I'll swim."

They leaped into the canal water, and he let himself sink down and down to the bottom like a golden statue and lie there in green silence. All was water-quiet and deep, all was peace. He felt the steady, slow current drift him easily.

If I lie here long enough, he thought, the water will work and eat away my flesh until the bones show like coral. Just my skeleton left. And then the water can build on that skeleton—green things, deep water things, red things, yellow things. Change. Change. Slow, deep, silent change. And isn't that what it is up *there?*

He saw the sky submerged above him, the sun made Martian by atmosphere and time and space.

Up there, a big river, he thought, a Martian river, all of us lying deep in it, in our pebble houses, in our sunken boulder houses, like crayfish hidden, and the water washing away our old bodies and lengthening the bones and—

He let himself drift up through the soft light.

Dan sat on the edge of the canal, regarding his father seriously.

"*Utha*," he said.

"What?" asked his father.

The boy smiled. "You know. *Utha*'s the Martian word for 'father.'"

"Where did you learn it?"

"I don't know. Around. *Utha!*"

"What do you want?"

The boy hesitated. "I—I want to change my name."

"Change it?"

"Yes."

His mother swam over. "What's wrong with Dan for a name?"

Dan fidgeted. "The other day you called Dan, Dan, Dan. I didn't even hear. I said to myself, That's not my name. I've a new name I want to use."

Mr. Bittering held to the side of the canal, his body cold and his heart pounding slowly. "What is this new name?"

"Linnl. Isn't that a good name? Can I use it? Can't I, please?"

Mr. Bittering put his hand to his head. He thought of the silly rocket, himself working alone, himself alone even among his family, so alone.

He heard his wife say, "Why not?"

He heard himself say, "Yes, you can use it."

"Yaaa!" screamed the boy. "I'm Linnl, Linnl!"

Racing down the meadowlands, he danced and shouted.

Mr. Bittering looked at his wife. "Why did we do that?"

"I don't know," she said. "It just seemed like a good idea."

They walked into the hills. They strolled on old mosaic paths, beside still pumping fountains. The paths were covered with a thin film of cool water all summer long. You kept your bare feet cool all the day, splashing as in a creek, wading.

They came to a small deserted Martian villa with a good view of the valley. It was on top of a hill. Blue marble halls, large murals, a swimming pool. It was refreshing in this hot summertime. The Martians hadn't believed in large cities.

"How nice," said Mrs. Bittering, "if we could move up here to this villa for the summer."

"Come on," he said. "We're going back to town. There's work to be done on the rocket."

But as he worked that night, the thought of the cool blue marble villa entered his mind. As the hours passed, the rocket seemed less important.

In the flow of days and weeks, the rocket receded and dwindled. The old fever was gone. It frightened him to think he had let it slip this way. But somehow the heat, the air, the working conditions—

He heard the men murmuring on the porch of his metal shop.

"Everyone's going. You heard?"

"All going. That's right."

Bittering came out. "Going where?" He saw a couple of trucks loaded with children and furniture, drive down the dusty street.

"Up to the villas," said the man.

"Yeah, Harry, I'm going. So is Sam. Aren't you, Sam?"

"That's right, Harry. What about you?"

"I've got work to do here."

"Work! You can finish that rocket in the autumn, when it's cooler."

He took a breath. "I got the frame all set up."

"In the autumn is better." Their voices were lazy in

the heat.

"Got to work," he said.

"Autumn," they reasoned. And they sounded so sensible, so right.

"Autumn would be best," he thought. "Plenty of time, then."

No! cried part of himself, deep down, put away, locked tight, suffocating. No! No!

"In the autumn," he said.

"Come on, Harry," they all said.

"Yes," he said, feeling his flesh melt in the hot liquid air. "Yes, in the autumn. I'll begin work again then."

"I got a villa near the Tirra Canal," said someone.

"You mean the Roosevelt Canal, don't you?"

"Tirra. The old Martian name."

"But on the map—"

"Forget the map. It's Tirra now. Now I found a place in the Pillan mountains—"

"You mean the Rockefeller range," said Bittering.

"I mean the Pillan mountains," said Sam.

"Yes," said Bittering, buried in the hot, swarming air. "The Pillan mountains."

Everyone worked at loading the truck in the hot, still afternoon of the next day.

Laura, Dan, and David carried packages. Or, as they preferred to be known, Ttil, Linnl, and Werr carried packages.

The furniture was abandoned in the little white cottage.

"It looked just fine in Boston," said the mother. "And here in the cottage. But up at the villa? No. We'll get it when we come back in the autumn."

Bittering himself was quiet.

"I've some ideas on furniture for the villa," he said after a time. "Big, lazy furniture."

"What about your encyclopedia? You're taking it along, surely?"

Mr. Bittering glanced away. "I'll come and get it next week."

They turned to their daughter. "What about your New York dresses?"

The bewildered girl stared. "Why, I don't want them any more."

They shut off the gas, the water, they locked the doors and walked away. Father peered into the truck.

"Gosh, we're not taking much," he said. "Considering all we brought to Mars, this is only a handful!"

He started the truck.

Looking at the small white cottage for a long moment, he was filled with a desire to rush to it, touch it, say good-by to it, for he felt as if he were going away on a long journey, leaving something to which he could never quite return, never understand again.

Just then Sam and his family drove by in another truck.

"Hi, Bittering! Here we go!"

The truck swung down the ancient highway out of town. There were sixty others traveling the same direction. The town filled with a silent, heavy dust from their passage. The canal waters lay blue in the sun, and a quiet wind moved in the strange trees.

"Good-by, town!" said Mr. Bittering.

"Good-by, good-by," said the family, waving to it.

They did not look back again.

Summer burned the canals dry. Summer moved like flame upon the meadows. In the empty Earth settlement, the painted houses flaked and peeled. Rubber tires upon which children had swung in back yards hung suspended like stopped clock pendulums in the blazing air.

At the metal shop, the rocket frame began to rust.

In the quiet autumn Mr. Bittering stood, very dark now, very golden-eyed, upon the slope above his villa, looking at the valley.

"It's time to go back," said Cora.

"Yes, but we're not going," he said quietly. "There's nothing there any more."

"Your books," she said. "Your fine clothes."

"Your *llles* and fine *ior uele rre*," she said.

"The town's empty. No one's going back," he said. "There's no reason to, none at all."

The daughter wove tapestries and the sons played songs on ancient flutes and pipes, their laughter echoing in the marble villa.

Mr. Bittering gazed at the Earth settlement far away in the low valley. "Such odd, such ridiculous houses the Earth people built."

"They didn't know any better," his wife mused. "Such ugly people. I'm glad they've gone."

They both looked at each other, startled by all they

had just finished saying. They laughed.

"Where did they go?" he wondered. He glanced at his wife. She was golden and slender as his daughter. She looked at him, and he seemed almost as young as their eldest son.

"I don't know," she said.

"We'll go back to town maybe next year, or the year after, or the year after that," he said, calmly. "Now—I'm warm. How about taking a swim?"

They turned their backs to the valley. Arm in arm they walked silently down a path of clear-running spring water.

Five years later a rocket fell out of the sky. It lay steaming in the valley. Men leaped out of it, shouting.

"We won the war on Earth! We're here to rescue you! Hey!"

But the American-built town of cottages, peach trees, and theaters was silent. They found a flimsy rocket frame rusting in an empty shop.

The rocket men searched the hills. The captain established headquarters in an abandoned bar. His lieutenant came back to report.

"The town's empty, but we found native life in the hills, sir. Dark people. Yellow eyes. Martians. Very friendly. We talked a bit, not much. They learn English fast. I'm sure our relations will be most friendly with them, sir."

"Dark, eh?" mused the captain. "How many?"

"Six, eight hundred, I'd say, living in those marble ruins in the hills, sir. Tall, healthy. Beautiful women."

"Did they tell you what became of the men and

women who built this Earth-settlement, Lieutenant?"

"They hadn't the foggiest notion of what happened to this town or its people."

"Strange. You think those Martians killed them?"

"They look surprisingly peaceful. Chances are a plague did this town in, sir."

"Perhaps. I suppose this is one of those mysteries we'll never solve. One of those mysteries you read about."

The captain looked at the room, the dusty windows, the blue mountains rising beyond, the canals moving in the light, and he heard the soft wind in the air. He shivered. Then, recovering, he tapped a large fresh map he had thumbtacked to the top of an empty table.

"Lots to be done, Lieutenant." His voice droned on and quietly on as the sun sank behind the blue hills. "New settlements. Mining sites, minerals to be looked for. Bacteriological specimens taken. The work, all the work. And the old records were lost. We'll have a job of remapping to do, renaming the mountains and rivers and such. Calls for a little imagination.

"What do you think of naming those mountains the Lincoln Mountains, this canal the Washington Canal, those hills—we can name those hills for you, Lieutenant. Diplomacy. And you, for a favor, might name a town for me. Polishing the apple. And why not make this the Einstein Valley, and further over . . . are you *listening*, Lieutenant?"

The lieutenant snapped his gaze from the blue color and the quiet mist of the hills far beyond the town.

"What? Oh, *yes*, sir!"

THE AMBASSADOR FROM EARTH

by Mari Eckstein Gower

I'd just bought a hotel for Boardwalk. That, along with my Park Place and St. James properties and railroads, put me in a pretty good position. I grinned at my perfect cousin, Elton. He adjusted the collar on his perfectly pressed polo shirt, brushed a perfect dark curl off his forehead, then picked up the dice, ready to roll.

The phone rang. Mom motioned, indicating it was for me.

"Be right back." I smiled. Let Elton contemplate losing for a change. I picked up the receiver. "Hello?"

"Potato alert."

"Not now, Jerry!" I whispered into the mouthpiece.

"I *said*, 'potato alert'!"

"I heard you." I glanced over at the Monopoly game. "Can't it wait?" I asked hopefully.

"Brian, it's important!"

"What's so important this time?"

"He's going to blow up the Space Needle."

I cast one last look at my string of hotels. Probably never, ever, in my entire life would I get another setup like that. With a resigned sigh, I said, "Be right there," then hung up the phone.

I smiled—this time, not so smugly—at Elton. "Sorry. I can't finish our game. A friend needs my help with something."

He smiled back. The thin silver line of his retainer gleamed, accentuating his newly perfect teeth. "May I come along?"

I struggled to hide my horror. "I don't think—"

Mom gave me her think-twice-about-that look.

"You'd be bored," I offered.

Mom frowned, switching to her that's-no-way-to-treat-a-guest stare.

Elton wasn't a guest. He was my cousin. But, knowing it'd be useless to argue, I added, "All right, come along."

Mom nodded her approval.

Trying to look cheerful, I pulled on my windbreaker. All the time, though, I wondered how I'd ditch Elton so I could save Seattle.

Now, I don't absolutely hate him or anything. It's just that he's taller, smarter, and handsomer than me. He's a star player in soccer, baseball, and tennis. Not only that, he keeps his room spotless. If I find a lucky penny in the street, he finds a lucky quarter. You get the idea.

While walking to Jerry's house, I devised a plan to sprint ahead and duck down a side street to lose him. Then I remembered, Elton could run much faster than me, too.

All right, on to Plan Two. Jerry and I would give Elton some impossible puzzle to solve. While he worked on it, we'd sneak out the back. No. Any puzzle Jerry and I'd come up with wouldn't stump genius Elton for long.

I'd just have to tell him the truth. "You've got to know something," I began as we passed beneath a long line of maple trees.

"What?"

"Well, you see, Jerry and I are working on a very important intergalactic problem."

"This is a joke, right?" he asked suspiciously.

"No. It's for real," I assured him. "An alien wants to destroy Seattle."

"Oh, I get it," said Elton sarcastically. "You're making up this dumb story to scare me off."

"That isn't it at all. He really wants to blow up Seattle—or, at least, the Space Needle."

"Okay. I give up." Elton snickered. "Why the Space Needle?"

"He's convinced it's some kind of weapon aimed at his planet." This sounded crazy, even to me. So I tried to elaborate, "You see, he's gotten a lot of things mixed up about Earth. Like he thinks Jerry and I are ambassadors negotiating a peace settlement with him."

"Oh yeah, alien as in from another planet."

"Yes," I replied, "Zoombutt is from the planet Zantor."

"Zoombutt! His name is Zoombutt?" Elton laughed.

I winced. "I know, I know. It doesn't translate well. But that's his name."

"Right," he said with a sneer. "So why haven't you turned this Zoombutt over to the police or the army?"

"Like I said, he's mixed up a lot of things. He thinks all adults are our slaves."

Elton shot me a withering look.

Ignoring his scorn, I continued. "When Zoombutt first arrived, he noticed how our parents drive us places, cook our meals, work to support us—all those sorts of things. So he came to the conclusion that they're our slaves." I cleared my throat. "He won't speak to adults because he's too important to deal with 'mere underlings.'"

Elton stared at me a moment. "I can't decide if you're completely deranged or the best storyteller I've ever heard."

"Look, I know this sounds strange. But Zoombutt really believes we've been assigned to negotiate with him."

"Right. And who gave you guys all this power?"

At this point I seriously considered lying. He already thought I was crazy. What difference would a little lie make? Problem was, it felt good to finally get this whole big mess off my chest.

"Jerry's cat, Suki."

Elton nearly spit out his retainer. "A *cat?*" he said, drawing out the word as if it were something foreign to him. "A real live cat?"

I nodded. Maybe I should've continued playing Monopoly and let the Space Needle blow up. He'd never understand why Zoombutt mistook Suki's natural aloofness for royal arrogance.

Elton laughed. He laughed so long and so hard that I began to worry. "Hey, I can play along," he said at last. "Let's meet this Zoombutt." He snickered. "Am I supposed to bow to the cat?"

"No," I replied evenly. "Just display proper respect and you'll be okay."

We walked in silence the rest of the way to Jerry's house. An uneasy feeling gnawed at me. Even though he'd acted like a jerk, shouldn't I prepare Elton more? After all, at first glance Zoombutt didn't appear . . . well, dangerous.

I glanced at Elton. He had an annoying, self-satisfied sneer plastered across his face. *Forget being a nice guy,* I thought. *Let him find out for himself.*

Jerry frowned when he opened the door. "You brought your cousin!"

"I couldn't—"

"—avoid bringing me," Elton said, as he pushed past Jerry. "So, where do you guys keep your little green man from outer space?"

"He isn't green," Jerry blurted out angrily. "And he's—oof!"

With a fast jab to Jerry's ribs, I finished, "—in the potting shed."

Jerry gave me a quizzical look.

As an afterthought, I added, "Probably conferring with the cat."

"You guys are real funny!" said Elton.

"Yeah!" I smiled sincerely. "It's a laugh a minute around here."

Jerry started to say something, but I motioned him to silence. "Come on, Elton," I said. "We'll show you the alien."

"Right," Elton said with a smirk.

Grabbing my cousin's elbow, I led him around the back of the house. "Here we are. Why don't you just peek through this crack. Let's not go in and disturb him."

"You think I'm dumb?" said Elton. "I want to inspect

this alien up close." With that, he yanked open the door and stomped into the shed.

"Sorry, cousin," I whispered as I slammed the door shut and locked it.

Elton yelled and banged the walls, but the lock held.

"What are you doing?" Jerry asked in a frightened tone.

"Aw, he'll be all right in there," I replied. "We'll let him out after we've dealt with Zoombutt."

Finally, Jerry caught on. "Oh, I see." He cast a regretful look back at the shed. "Too bad about your cousin, though. Your mom'll have a fit when she finds out what you've done to him."

"Yeah. But that's nothing compared to what she'd do if I let him get you-know-what."

"You're right." Jerry sighed. "It's safer this way."

Turning back toward Jerry's house, we passed a row of garden statues. *Looks like he's added a few squirrels*, I thought while surveying the odd assortment of wildlife. *Pretty soon someone's bound to notice.*

As we crossed the lawn, the neighbor's Yorkshire terrier, Binkie, rushed out at us. "Yap, yap, yap! Yap, yap, yap!"

"Quiet!" whispered Jerry. "Ow!"

After nipping his ankle, Binkie continued. "Yap, yap, yap!"

"Hey," I growled. "Quiet or I'll call the cat."

That got him. After a few halfhearted yaps, Binkie scrambled back into his own yard.

Jerry raised his pant leg. "I think he's broken the skin."

"We'll deal with that later," I told him. "How serious is the threat this time?"

"Pretty serious. He's playing with that Transmogrifier machine-thing of his. When I left, he was calculating wind velocity."

I sighed. "This is out of control. We'd better come to a final peace settlement soon. I can't handle many more of these emergencies."

"Me neither," agreed Jerry.

No one in Jerry's family used their garage. What with all the old furniture, filing cabinets, and assorted junk, they had no room left for a car. In other words, the ideal hideout.

When we arrived, we found Zoombutt pacing from one end of the garage to the other. It was a pretty weird sight. Since his legs were so short, he kind of rolled more than walked. And, whenever he passed the paint compressor, his tiny arms waved up and down. I couldn't tell if he was arguing with the tools or just mumbling to himself.

Either way, I silently congratulated myself. Elton was much better off in the potting shed. One look at Zoombutt, and he'd surely do something stupid. Not that I'd blame him. You see, Zoombutt looked a bit like a three-foot-high potato with huge eyes and a big, bulbous nose. Most normal humans would find him funnylooking. Until they learned about his temper, that is.

Zoombutt stopped rolling and swiveled around to face us. "I am dismayed," he said in his helium-toned, squeaky voice.

"So sorry we're late, Commander." I bowed low. "But—"

"I try and I try," he continued, "and still your ruler greets me with disdain."

Jerry's cat, Suki, sat on the shelf next to the painting supplies. Her deep green eyes narrowed to slits as her tail swished with annoyance.

How could I explain that disdain was the best you ever got from that cat? Instead, I tried to smooth things over. "Our ruler is not amused by your threats to destroy her favorite plaything."

"Plaything! Plaything!" Zoombutt's voice rose to a hysterical squeal. "Your crude attempts at humor do not mislead me, Ambassador. I know the true intent of your tower!"

Jerry nudged my elbow. "See what I mean?" he whispered. "He won't believe me when—"

"I hear your plotting!" squeeked Zoombutt.

"We were just conferring about—"

"Your crude communication mode is of no interest to me. Not when Zantor's safety is in jeopardy!"

"I understand your concern." For lack of anything better to do, I bowed again. "But that tower is merely a form of entertainment—"

"Enough! I've seen your slaves traveling up and down the energy shaft. I've seen its night beacon."

Jerry and I exchanged glances.

"I am not deceived," continued Zoombutt.

"We never thought—" started Jerry.

"Aha! So you admit it!"

"What I meant," wailed Jerry, "is it's only—"

Someone began clapping behind me. "Very good,"

boomed Elton's voice. "Very, very good."

I turned around. At that moment, my always-perfect cousin didn't look quite so perfect. Cobwebs clung to his tousled hair. Dirt and grease covered his face, shirt, and hands.

"You should have stayed in the shed, Elton," I said wearily.

"And missed this performance? No way, cousin. Why, your Mr. Potato robot alone is worth the price of admission. Bravo!" He continued clapping. "Are you manipulating it by strings? Or does it have a remote control?"

Zoombutt shot me an accusing look. "Who is this interloper?"

"Ignore him, Commander. He's merely my cousin."

"Cousin? What is this word, 'cousin'?"

I took a deep breath. "This cousin," I explained patiently, "is the offspring of my female parent's sibling. On Earth we call them family. It is our custom to make allowances for our family member's odd behavior."

Zoombutt scrutinized Elton, clearly considering him a lower life-form. "I understand this custom. I, too, must tolerate family members of substandard intelligence."

"Hey!" grumbled Elton.

"Stay out of the way and keep quiet," I warned under my breath.

But Elton wasn't about to do either. "No potato robot is going to insult me," he said loudly.

"Your loathsome family member appears to have serious defects in its thinking apparatus," said Zoombutt.

"All right," growled Elton. "I tried being a good sport with you guys, even after you locked me in that dark, dirty shed. I wanted you to accept me. But no more! I've had it!"

I'd never seen him like this. Usually he acted cool and in control. "Calm down," I said.

"Calm down, yourself!" yelled Elton. "I'm tired of you belittling everything I do."

That did it. "Well, *I'm* tired," I yelled back, "of always being compared to Mr. Perfect!"

"Ah, yes," observed Zoombutt. "We have similar family member discussions on Zantor."

"I can't help it if you're compared to me!" shouted Elton. "How do you think *I* feel, watching Mr. Popular rush off to do interesting things with his friends? Do you think I enjoy being everyone's second choice?"

Mr. Popular? Me?

Before I could comment, Zoombutt interjected, "Perhaps we should adjust its thinking synapses." He began pressing buttons and turning dials on his Transmogrifier. "A few minor adjustments will augment—"

"Give me that stupid thing!" Elton snatched the machine out of his hands, then raced out of the garage.

Zoombutt turned green with rage. "Your family member has malfunctioned beyond repair!" He grabbed his blaster and chased after Elton.

Jerry and I stared at each other in disbelief.

"Yap, yap, yap!" We heard Binkie barking like a maniac in the backyard.

"Traitors! Ambush!" shouted Zoombutt. "Your troops shall not trap me!"

ZAP blat blat blat blat blat!

"Oh no!" Jerry and I cried in unison and ran outside.

But the damage was already done. Binkie stood, petrified mid-yap. Near him were two stiffened squirrels, a couple of blue jays, and a frog with a very surprised expression on its face.

"Uh oh," I muttered under my breath. "More garden sculptures."

Lucky as always, Elton had missed being zapped in the skirmish.

Zoombutt fumbled with the buttons on the side of his blaster.

"Now's our chance," whispered Jerry. "Let's get out of here before he recharges that thing."

But I couldn't leave my cousin. And, at that moment, poor Elton didn't look like he was going anywhere fast. He pointed at the Binkie-statue, stuttering, "He . . . he just . . . zap! . . . and . . . blat! . . . and then dog . . . FROZEN!"

"Fossilized would be more accurate," I corrected. "Or petrified or mineralized or—"

"Brian," wheezed Jerry. "Let's get out of here."

"Never did like that dog," I added.

"Brian, please! He could start blasting again."

Jerry was right. We had to act fast or I'd have a heck of a lot of explaining to do. Mom would hate it if I let an alien fossilize my cousin.

Not that Elton helped matters much. He continued

staring at Binkie, mumbling to himself. Suddenly, I felt sorry for him. No matter how big a pain he might be, he didn't deserve being petrified.

The blaster emitted a high-pitched whine.

I needed a diversion. Anything to take Zoombutt's mind off Elton. I noticed Suki stalking a bird on the far side of the yard. If I could get her attention . . . but, no. Suki was no dummy. She wouldn't trade a nice plump bird for a few pats on the head.

Meanwhile, Zoombutt aimed his blaster straight at Elton.

Poor Elton turned pale. His jaw dropped. And then his retainer fell from his mouth, hitting the grass with a tiny *plunk.*

Zoombutt glanced at the twisted metal and plastic lying on the lawn. "What has your loathsome relative been concealing?" he asked as he picked up the retainer and inspected it.

My stomach did a triple flip. We were sunk, absolutely sunk.

Zoombutt sniffed Elton's retainer. A tiny glob of spit slowly dripped from the mouthpiece.

I contemplated my future as a piece of lawn statuary.

But instead of the blaster's shrill zap, I heard a contented little sigh. Zoombutt couldn't hide his excitement as he eagerly turned the retainer this way and that, examining every detail.

What was going on? "I hate to disturb you, Commander—" I said.

Clutching the retainer protectively against his chest,

he attempted a nonchalant pose. "Where did you find this . . . artifact?"

Jerry laughed. "Oh, it's just—ouch!"

I stomped down hard on his foot. "You know how it is," I said, trying to sound cool and witty, like movie heroes always do when they're bargaining with the bad guy. But my voice cracked as I added, "They turn up here, there—"

Zoombutt was too busy cuddling the retainer to notice my nervousness. "You wouldn't happen to have any more of these?" he asked casually.

"Oh, yeah—" said Jerry.

I quickly interrupted. "Of course, they aren't easy to find. I'll need my assistant, there—" I indicated Elton "—to help me."

"Ah! I understand," said Zoombutt. "The family business."

I nodded.

"Odious as they can be at times, family has its uses," he said. Then his eyes took on a sly glint. "May I take this item to Zantor? For study! Purely for scientific study!"

"One must make sacrifices," I said, "to fulfill family obligations."

Zoombutt chuckled. "Your ruler is truly wise to choose such a clever negotiator." Then he got that shrewd, almost sneaky, look again. "So I must leave now."

"What about the Space Needle?" asked Jerry.

I kicked him, but not in time.

Zoombutt's tiny fingers drummed lovingly on the

retainer. "Unfortunately, pressing matters await me on Zantor. For the moment, I am willing to overlook your Space Needle. But I shall return."

"I understand," I replied.

Zoombutt cackled with glee. Then, tapping the retainer, he said in a conspiratorial tone, "This will purchase a handsome spacecraft on Zantor."

"I'm sure it will," I said, managing to keep a serious face.

"But, you can't leave Binkie like this!" cried Jerry.

Zoombutt studied the little Binkie-statue. "Yes, a most valiant warrior." He thought a moment, then giggled. "What a spacecraft I shall build! I feel magnanimous, so"—he pressed the side panel of his blaster and zapped Binkie—"I give you back your comrade."

Gradually, Binkie melted back to his real-life colors. He shook himself, then tried to yap. No sound came out.

"Unfortunately," said Zoombutt with sincere regret, "the reversal process affects the voice generator. I am afraid that, henceforth, his communication skills shall be seriously limited."

"We'll manage," I replied dryly.

"I must leave now," Zoombutt said with undisguised haste. "I can't wait! My spacecraft shall have a moonroom and a sand-bathing area . . ."

He picked up the Transmogrifier, adjusted a few dials, then disappeared in a beam of yellow light.

"Whew!" said Jerry. "I can't believe it!"

"Me neither," I said.

At our feet, Binkie continued silently yapping. He looked like one of those mimes who pretend they're trapped inside an invisible box.

"I think I like him better this way," I said.

"Yeah," agreed Jerry. "But what about your cousin?"

Elton hadn't moved. He still had that pale, sick look on his face.

"Elton?" I shook him. "Elton? Come on. Snap out of it!"

"Huh?"

"Everything's all right, now," I said.

"You tricked that space guy to save me."

"Well, yeah. I guess I did."

He gave me a big bear hug. "You must actually like me."

What could I say? Of course I liked him. He was family.

"But what will you do when Zoombutt returns?"

"That's right," chimed in Jerry. "What are we going to do?"

"Do? Well, first thing, we'll need more retainers," I said, already laying out a plan.

It suddenly struck me: I'd developed a real knack for interplanetary negotiations. One thing was certain, though. Zoombutt would have to show a little more respect if he wanted a good deal next time.

In Our Hands

by Bruce Coville

I'm totally freaked out. But that is probably true for everyone on the planet, except maybe people living in the deep rain forest or something. How could we not be, after what happened this morning?

I was sitting at the kitchen table, arguing with Mom about how much sugar I could put on my cereal when it started. The television made this weird sound. Looking up, I forgot all about the sugar.

The dweeby news anchor had been replaced by a woman who had blue skin and green hair. Her ears seemed much too small for her head, her eyes much too big. I laughed, because it was kind of cool, and I figured some idiot at the station was playing a joke, or had made a weird mistake.

"Someone's going to be in big trouble for this," predicted Mom. "I bet they get fired."

We stared at the screen, waiting for the news to come back on. (I was only watching the news because it's an assignment for social studies class.) Nothing happened. Finally, I picked up the remote and changed the channel.

The woman was still there.

I changed it again, and again, and again.

No matter what channel I turned to—and we get forty-seven of them—the blue woman was still there.

My mother's eyes got wider, and she slid her chair closer to mine. I felt something weird—some combination of fear and excitement—begin to blossom in my stomach.

Finally the woman spoke: "Greetings, people of Earth."

Mom shook her head in disgust. "What a stupid joke," she muttered.

My skin began to prickle. What kind of joke could put a person on forty-seven channels at the same time?

The blue woman continued to speak. "What I have to tell you now will not make sense unless you know two things."

As far as I was concerned, nothing made sense right now.

"First, we are not here to threaten you."

It was such an odd thing to say I almost laughed. But part of me was too scared for that. I wished that Dad were here. I knew I would feel better if he was with us. But Dad was gone, a victim of the air crisis that had killed so many people the year I was three.

The blue woman spoke again. "Second, you must know that we can do what we say. I will now prove that to you. Please do not be frightened. This demonstration is just to help you accept the truth of what I have to tell you."

Mom reached for her coffee. Her hand was shaking, which only made me feel more frightened. Before she could pick up her cup, the light went out. Not the lights. The light. Darkness was everywhere, as if the sun itself had disappeared. I cried out in fright, in astonishment.

"Do not be afraid," said the voice from the TV, as if it had heard me. "We will return the light soon."

I wondered how the TV could work with the power out, until I understood that this was not a power loss. It was a light loss.

Suddenly, the light did come back. I rubbed my eyes and blinked.

"If you can go outside, please do so," said the blue woman. I don't like to go outside if I can help it; the air is too dirty, and it hurts my lungs. But I went. So did Mom. So did most of the people in our development.

A humming sound filled the sky. I looked up and gasped. The sky was filled with enormous red ships. They hovered there, not moving, as if suspended by invisible cables.

"This is the Vegan Starfleet," boomed the voice, which now seemed to come directly from the sky. "It comes in peace."

If you come in peace, then why are there so many of you? I wondered.

Some people cried. Others screamed. The man next to me crossed himself. The man next to him fainted. I could feel Mom's hand tighten on my shoulder.

"Please do not panic," said the voice. "Go back to your homes. We have wonders to show you."

Slowly, people drifted inside. Ann, my mother's friend from next door, came in with us. She was crying. The television was showing pictures of the Vegan Starfleet. A news announcer came on. He looked terrified.

"The reports we are seeing indicate that the Vegan

fleet which suddenly appeared in our skies is so vast it can be seen from every spot on the planet. The president has said—"

The screen blinked. The announcer disappeared and the blue-skinned woman took his place.

"Forgive us if we have frightened you. But you must understand our power before you can understand our offer."

I put my hands on the table to try to stop them from trembling.

"They can do anything," whispered Ann, her voice thick with horror.

The picture changed. A beautiful world appeared on the screen. "This is our home," said the alien. Then she showed us picture after picture of clean cities, happy people, great forests. No one looked hungry. No one seemed sick.

"Now," said the Vegan, "let me tell you why we are here. You have many troubles: war . . . poverty . . . hunger . . . terrorism."

As she spoke, ugly images flowed across the screen. I saw young men and women, some of them no older than me, dying in battle; I saw children lying on dusty streets, their bellies swollen with hunger; I saw bombs exploding among rushing crowds. More pictures followed: a forest, yellow and dying; a dead river, thick with sludge; the remains of Chicago. I had seen all this before, of course. But now I felt my cheeks grow hot with shame. I didn't like to have visitors from another world know about these things. I was embarrassed because I knew we should have done more to fix them.

"Do not feel bad," said the Vegan, as if she were reading my mind. "Once we had these problems, too. But we have solved them. That is why we have come: to offer you our solutions." Her face appeared on the screen again, smiling and gentle.

"Think of it," she said. "With our help you can end war, hunger, and disease. We have cures for the mind and the body that can take you to a Golden Age."

"But what do they want in return?" asked Ann. She was looking right at me, as if I would have the answer. I shook my head. I didn't know.

"Here is the choice we bring you," said the Vegan. "We will teach you what we know. Or we will leave, and let you find it out for yourselves, as we did. But you must understand that you may not live through the process. Your world has reached a danger point. You have too many bombs. You have too many weapons. You may destroy the planet before you heal yourselves.

"However what we offer is also dangerous—tools and powers greater than any you now possess. If we simply gave them to you, we have little doubt that you would destroy yourself within ten years.

"Therefore, we offer this trade: put yourselves in our hands. Let us care for your world, until you are ready to do the job properly. You will have to give up making your own laws, of course. We will do that for you. We will run your schools. We will decide what your factories make. We will distribute the products.

"In return, we will give you amazing new tools. We will clean your water and take the poison from your air. We will feed your hungry, cloth your poor, heal your sick." She smiled. "Of course, you could do these things yourself, if you really wanted to. But then, you already know that, don't you?"

The Vegan stopped smiling. "The choice you face is too important to be made by politicians. It must be made by the people—all the people. This, too, we can make possible.

"Soon, you will fall into a deep sleep. After you do, we will prepare you for the vote. When that is done, we will leave, so that you can think about our offer. In eight days, we will return. Then, it will be time for you to vote. If you reject our offer, that will be the end of it. We will leave in peace. If you choose to accept our offer, we will begin work immediately."

Her voice was kind. Even so, I began to shake as I felt myself grow sleepy. I reached for my mother. She moved closer to me.

When I woke, my head was lying on the table. Mom was still beside me. Her right hand lay open on the table. In her palm was a strip of something shiny and blue. I looked at my own hand. I had a strip, too. I ran my finger over it. It felt like part of my own skin, almost as if it had grown there. I looked at the strip more closely. It was about a half-an-inch wide, and an inch long. At each end was a black circle about the size of my fingertip.

193

Inside one circle was the word "YES."

Inside the other it said "NO."

Mom and Ann woke a few seconds later. We walked outside. The sky was empty. The Vegans had gone.

"Do you believe them?" asked Mom.

I shook my head. "I don't know. I don't know what to believe."

Other people were coming out of their homes. Everyone was talking. Fights broke out—first with words, then with fists. I was glad the Vegans had gone. I didn't want them to see this.

We went back inside. The president was on television, making a speech about what the country would do to put an end to the alien menace. But it was just words. The Vegans were too powerful for us. I knew it. The president knew it. Everyone knew it.

Besides, I wasn't sure they were a menace. After all, with their advanced science they could simply have taken over. But they didn't. So maybe the choice really was up to us. I looked at my hand and began to laugh.

"What's so funny?" asked Ann sharply.

I showed her my open palm. "The Vegans have made a joke," I said. "For the first time in history, our future really is in our own hands!"

July 23

Mom and I went to the town hall today. It was jammed with hundreds of people who had come to talk about the Vegan Proposal.

"I was in the last war," shouted a man. "I fought to protect our freedom. I didn't want other people making choices for me then, and I don't want it now. I say 'No!' to the Vegans."

"I was in the war, too," said a tall woman. "I saw men and women lose their legs, their arms, their eyes. I saw children with the skin burned off their bodies. I know we don't need another war. I say 'Yes' to the Vegans."

"They'll make us slaves!" yelled someone behind me.

"They could do that without a vote," said someone else. Other people began shouting, until the place was ringing with voices. It took several minutes for the mayor to bring the meeting back to order.

"Look at us," said another man, once things had settled down. "We aren't hungry, or poor. Most of us live long, healthy lives. Why should we give control to the Vegans?"

But what about the others? I wondered. *What about the millions who are sick and poor and dying? Should we vote no just because we're comfortable?*

The debate went on all day. Tonight, the television showed more debates, from around the country, and around the world. Demonstrations were raging in most cities, with opposing mobs carrying signs like "Nuke the Vegans!" and "Vote Vegan—It's Our Only Hope!"

July 27

Mom hasn't gone to work for the last two days. She said she couldn't see any point in it. Nothing gets done. All anyone can talk about, think about, is the Vegan Proposal.

July 30

Last night, a huge screen appeared in the center of town. According to the news, screens just like it have appeared on every block of every city in the world. They have appeared in every town, every village, no matter how small, no matter how remote. They are tally screens. This afternoon, they will record the votes of six billion people as we choose whether we will rule our own future, or give control to the Vegans.

Some people are angry that the Vegans are letting kids vote, too. They say this should be just for adults. But they can't figure any way to keep us from voting. (Though I figure in some places grown-ups will grab kids' hands and vote for them.) But I don't see why we shouldn't vote. It's our world, too. It's our future, even more than the grown-ups', since we're going to be living in it longer.

I've been taking it very seriously, but my mind is spinning with all I have heard this week, all the words about the poor and the sick and the dying; about freedom and power and dignity.

I don't want aliens to run our world. But when I look around, when I see what a mess it is, when I think of the bombs that can end all life, I feel afraid. I don't know if we are grown up enough to take care of ourselves.

Last night, Mom got out the family album, and we spent a lot of time looking at pictures. I stared at the photos of Dad, who I miss so much. I believe he would still be alive, if we had had Vegan science. But what would Dad have said about all this? He was a proud man, as I remember him. Proud and stubborn. Would he have wanted to live under someone else's rule?

Do I?

July 31

I am sitting in my room, staring at the strip in my hand. I am thinking of all I have seen, all I have done, all I want to do. I am thinking of the last time I saw Dad, cold and still in his coffin, and how Vegan medicine might have saved him—how Vegan science might have prevented the air crisis, and saved so many others like him.

I think of our glory and our despair. I think of all we do to one another in the name of love, of peace, of freedom, of God—all the good, and all the bad. I think of how far we have come in just a few thousand years. I think of how far there is to go and how many people will suffer and die before we get there.

I think of the stars, and the worlds out there waiting for us to join them.

I think of all these things, and I wonder what I will do in five minutes when the Vegans ask me to choose between the riches they offer and the freedom to find our own sad and starry path.

I look at the strip in my hand, at the YES and the NO, and I wonder.

ABOUT THE AUTHORS:

MEL GILDEN is the author of many children's books, including the *My Brother Blubb* and *Fifth Grade Monster* series. He's also perpetrated novelizations of stories from *Beverly Hills 90210*, and written two *Star Trek* novels. Mel lives in Los Angeles, California, and still hopes to be an astronaut when he grows up.

LOIS TILTON is the author of *Vampire Winter* and several dozen other works of fantasy and science fiction. One of her stories appeared in *Bruce Coville's Book of Spine-Tinglers*. She lives near Chicago, Illinois, where she is currently working on a novel based on ancient Greek history.

EDWARD D. HOCH is a past president of the Mystery Writers of America and winner of its Edgar Award for Best Short Story in 1968. He has published over 800 short stories and nearly 50 novels, collections, and anthologies. Ed lives in Rochester, New York, with his wife, Patricia.

ESTHER M. FRIESNER is an award-winning SF and fantasy author who has taken the time between wardrobe overhauls to write over twenty-five books, one hundred short stories, and to keep her family, cats, and househamster informed of the latest trends in haute couture.

CAROL OTTOLENGHI-BARGA's science fiction, tall tales, and historical adventure stories for kids have been published in many magazines, including *Cricket*, *Faces*, and *Spider*. She lives in Ohio with her husband, two sports-loving kids, a dog, and a three-year-old goldfish named Piggy.

LOU GRINZO is a computer programmer and technical writer who authored the book *Zen of Windows '95 Programming*. He lives in beautiful upstate New York with his wife, Liz.

MARC BILGREY has written for TV, magazines, and comedians. His short stories have appeared in numerous anthologies including *Phantoms of the Night*, *First Contact*, and *Cat Crimes Through Time*.

SHERWOOD SMITH lives in California. She started writing about another world when she was eight, and hasn't stopped since. She has stories in several anthologies, and has published two fantasy novels for young readers: *Wren to the Rescue* and *Wren's Quest*.

DEBORAH WHEELER started telling stories as a small child and kept on writing. She's written two novels—*Jaydium* and *Northlight*—and around three dozen short stories, one of which appeared in the *Star Wars* anthology *Tales from Jabba's Palace*. Deborah lives in Los Angeles.

LAWRENCE WATT-EVANS is the author of a couple of dozen novels and over a hundred short stories, including more than half a dozen that have appeared in previous Bruce Coville anthologies. He's a full-time writer living in Maryland with his wife, two kids, a cat, and a hamster.

ALETHEA EASON lives in Lake County, California with her husband, Bill. She's had stories published in *Marion Zimmer Bradley's Fantasy Magazine*, *New Moon Magazine*, *Shoofly*, and most recently in the anthology *A Glory of Unicorns*, edited by Bruce Coville.

RAY BRADBURY lives in Los Angeles. He sold his first story over fifty years ago, when he was only twenty. Still actively writing, he is beloved throughout the world as one of the most poetic science fiction writers of all time.

MARI ECKSTEIN GOWER lives in the Pacific Northwest with her husband, James, their two children, and a cowardly Corgi named Feather. When Mari isn't writing or painting, she enjoys gardening, yoga, hiking, and watching "bad" movies.

ABOUT THE ARTISTS:

ERNIE COLÓN, cover artist, has worked on a wide variety of comic book-related projects during the course of his long career, including *Scooby Doo*, the *Star Wars* tie-in *Droids*, and *Richie Rich* and *Casper, the Friendly Ghost*. Ernie lives on Long Island, New York, with his wife and daughter.

ALEX SUNDER, pencil artist for the story illustrations, received national recognition in his native Brazil as the creator and penciller of the popular comic book *Godless*. When he's not busily working away on comics, Alex pursues his two favorite hobbies: music and surfing the Internet.

JOHN NYBERG, who inked the story illustrations, has been a comic book artist for 14 years; among his many accomplishments are *Green Arrow*, *The Flash*, and *WildC.A.T.S*. John lives in New Jersey with his wife, Amy, and their two cats, Bart and Lisa.

BRUCE COVILLE was born in Syracuse, New York, and grew up in a rural area north of the city, around the corner from his grandparents' dairy farm. He lives in a brick house in Syracuse with his wife, his youngest child, three cats, and a dog named Thor. Though he has been a teacher, a toymaker, and a gravedigger, he prefers writing. His dozens of books for young readers include the bestselling *My Teacher Is an Alien* series, *Goblins in the Castle*, *Aliens Ate My Homework*, and *Sarah's Unicorn*.